my love my legacy

Traditional Chinese and Western Recipes for My Children

Grace Chiu

This book is created and published in April 2011, by Grace Chiu in Danville, California

Cover Designer ♥ Cheston Chiu

Photographers ♥ Michael Chen
♥ Bill Chen
♥ Julie Wang

Printed and bound in China

ISBN 978-1-4507-6395-0

$16.95 U.S.

my love, my legacy:

Traditional Chinese
and Western Recipes
for my Children
Grace Chiu

Dear Clyde,

Bon Appétit.

Grace Chiu

To Cynthia and Annjoe,
Cheston and Angie,
Connie and Albert.

Contents

Introduction

I never dreamed that I would be teaching cooking classes and writing my own book of recipes after I retired from the business world. However I have always been interested in food and I love to eat! I most likely have inherited this from my parents. Because of my passion for food, which began as a link to my heritage as an immigrant in the U.S., cooking became a form of relaxation therapy from the pressures at work and the stress from raising a family.

My cooking interest began when I was in graduate school in the U.S. Away from home and homesick, I missed the family gatherings we used to have where delicious meals prepared by my mother would be enjoyed. My parents were born in Shanghai and immigrated to Taiwan in the late 1940's. They often told me that the cuisine and dim sum in Shanghai were the best in the world. I have fond childhood memories of many great dishes my mother made during certain Chinese festivals and other special occasions throughout the year. My mother was highly regarded for her cooking despite never having had any professional culinary training.

Growing up in Taiwan, I was indoctrinated in the traditional social value system. My parents counseled me to study hard in order to achieve academic excellence. Domestic skills such as cooking or sewing were deemphasized. As a result I rarely had a chance to cook in Taiwan. After college I came to the United States for graduate school. That's when I started to learn western cooking. First, I picked up basic cooking skills from my advisor's wife and my coworkers in the work-study program. Then I started to explore different as well as more advanced cooking techniques.

During my years in graduate school, I studied diligently,

yet, spent my free time in kitchen practicing cooking. I enjoyed cooking very much especially when my family and friends praised and appreciated the delicious meals I had created. I have to thank many people who encouraged me to cook. Among them are Mrs. Jackie Brooks, my advisor's wife, and Mrs. Beth West, my department secretary – both of whom were wonderful cooking teachers. Many of the western dishes in this book were developed while I was in graduate school, and were critiqued by friends and schoolmates. Of course, each dish has evolved through the years to incorporate people's tastes, presentation style, and nutrition trends.

In the mid-1980s, my family and I moved from a Mountain State to a Coastal State, specifically the San Francisco Bay Area. What a blessing to have access to large varieties of fresh produce and well stocked Asian supermarkets! The ingredients that were never available are now within my reach and plentiful. So I started cooking Chinese dishes and re-creating my mother's favorite recipes. Not only did I follow my mother's three main principles of cooking: harmony in color, smell, and taste, but I also, drew upon my western cooking influence and I added my own culinary variations to her recipes.

Spending time in the kitchen has been wonderful for my family and me. Sharing the joys of great food became part of our social activities in California; friendship and food were easily linked. However, every working mother faces the challenge of balancing family life and work obligations, especially when children are young. I found enjoyment and relief from the stresses of living in a big city and endless office deadlines through cooking. As soon as I entered the kitchen and started making dinner for my family, the stresses disappeared.

In 2008 Ms. Julie Wang, the president of Taipei First Girls

High School Alumnae Association of Northern California (TFGHAA) approached me about teach cooking classes for local alumnae through the school website. I jumped at the opportunity. I wanted to share with them my enthusiasm for the art of cooking and, just as important, to leave a legacy for my children. I hope my children learn these family recipes and pass on to future generations.

Since 2008 TFGHAA has posted my recipes along with the respective cooking videos for two dishes each month. This cookbook contains a collection of more than ninety recipes previously demonstrated in my classes. The book also embraces my philosophy in cooking with these three principles:

♦ Simple preparation with easy steps to follow.

♦ Retain the original flavors of ingredients, which when combined together will result in healthy and delicious dishes.

♦ Prepare enough food for one meal plus leftovers, to save time and money.

Many of the recipes are designed for dinner with the family. Home-style cooking has served as a healthy and economical food source and built our family bond. Other recipes are for special occasions and require a little more time and some special ingredients. However, many of the quick dishes can be modified for entertaining simply by changing the presentation or increasing the quantity.

This cookbook is divided into two sections (each with a table of contents): first, popular and traditional Chinese dishes, followed by everyday easy western meals. My hope is that this book can help those who are learning to cook as well as those who are just searching for new ideas. I encourage the reader to modify the recipes based on his or her own preferences for ingredients, taste and presentation. I hope these recipes will bring families together at mealtime, which I believe is one of the most important experiences a family can share.

In publishing this cookbook, I would like to thank Ms. Julie Wang who helped me discover a new pastime that involves an activity I feel very passionate about. I would also like to thank Ms. JP Shaw and her husband, Mr. Bill Chen, and their son, Michael, who took videos of my cooking demonstrations and photos of the resulting dishes. Of course, I would like to thank my husband, YuHsing, and my children, Cynthia and Cheston, and my sister Ivy, who gave their support and encouragement, and willingly served as my taste-testers. I would especially like to thank my niece Ms. Connie Yu, my friends, Margaret Huang and Rose Chen for their valuable comments and many hours editing and proofreading this book.

Enjoy! Happy Cooking!

Grace Chiu

Danville, California

7

Traditional Chinese Cuisine

A. Cold Dish（冷盤）

Noodle Salad in Peanut Butter Sauce*	12
Cold Smoked Fish Shanghai Style	14
Shredded Carrot and Celery Salad*	16
Shredded Turnips and Jellyfish Salad	18
Veggie Goose*	20

B. Main Course（主菜）

Braised Pork Shoulder	22
Chinese New Year Tuan-Yuan Hot Pot Soup	24
Cod Fillet Rolls in Sweet and Sour Sauce	28
Diced Chicken with Assorted Peppers	30
Ground Meat Bean Curd Rolls	32
Kung Pao Chicken	34
Lion's Head Meatballs	36
Ma-Po (Spicy) Tofu	38
Minced Shrimp in Lettuce Wrap	40
Sautéed Prawn with Tomato Sauce	42
Paper Wrapped Chicken	44
Sautéed Mixed Vegetables*	46
Shredded Pork Tenderloin and Bean Sheet Delight	48
Steamed Pearl Balls	50
Steamed Whole Fish in Microwave Oven	52
Stir-Fried Assorted Vegetables*	54
Stir-Fried Beef with Asparagus	56
Veggie Yellow Birds*	58
Wuxi Style Pork Ribs	60

Gourmet Western Meals

E. Quick Fix

F. Main Course

(*) : vegetarian dish.

Noodle Salad
in Peanut Butter Sauce

Ingredients: *(makes 10 to 12 servings)*

- ♥ 1 pound spaghetti
- ♥ 1 medium size English cucumber, shredded
- ♥ 1 carrot, shredded
- ♥ 1 cup bean sprouts
- ♥ 1 yellow or orange pepper, sliced (optional)
- ♥ 1 tablespoon chopped fresh cilantro
- ♥ 3 tablespoons toasted peanuts, chopped (optional)

Dressing:
- ♥ 1/3 cup extra virgin olive oil
- ♥ 2 tablespoons rice wine vinegar
- ♥ 1/4 cup soy sauce
- ♥ 3 tablespoons sesame oil
- ♥ 1 tablespoon honey
- ♥ 1/2 cup or more smooth peanut butter
- ♥ 2 stalks green onions, minced
- ♥ 1 teaspoon grated fresh ginger

花生醬涼麵

Cooking Steps:

1. Bring a large pot of water to boil. Cook the spaghetti according to package directions. Drain and transfer to a big bowl, toss it with a little of extra virgin olive oil, minced green onion and grated ginger immediately.

2. For the dressing, whisk together the oil, rice wine vinegar, soy sauce, sesame oil, honey, ginger, peanut butter, and green onion.

3. Blanch bean sprouts in boiling water for 30 seconds, drain and squeeze dry.

4. Spread vegetables, carrots, cucumber, bean sprouts and peppers, evenly on top of the noodle; pour the dressing over and mix them well.

5. Sprinkle 2 tablespoons crushed peanuts and decorate with some chopped cilantros or green onions.

6. This is a great vegetarian dish in summer.

Cold Smoked Fish

Ingredients: *(makes 8 servings)*

- 11/2 pounds golden pompano fish or any white fish with firm meat
- 1 teaspoon five spice powder
- 2 to 3 tablespoons brown sugar
- 2 tablespoons rice vinegar
- Cooking oil for frying

Marinade:

- 3 stalks green onions, chopped
- 1 ginger, sliced
- 1/2 cup dark soy sauce
- 1/4 cup white wine
- 1 teaspoon salt

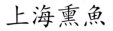

Cooking Steps:

1. Cut fish into 3.5"x2"x1" steaks.

2. Marinate fish with marinade sauce for two hours or overnight.

3. Heat oil in a deep sauté pan with high heat; fry the fish until golden brown about 5 to 6 minutes. Transfer fish steaks to a plate with paper towels and let oil drain and dry.

4. Heat the marinade sauce, add rice vinegar, sugar and the five spice powder. Cook it a few minutes until the flavors are combined. Return fish steaks back into the sauce and cook for 3 minutes until each fish steak is coated with sauce.

5. Taste for seasoning. Turn off the heat and transfer fish to a plate, let it cool.

6. It's better to serve smoked fish in cold; you may combine it with Turnips and Jellyfish Salad as a cold appetizer platter.

7. It can be stored in refrigerator up to one week.

Shredded Carrot and Celery Salad

Ingredients: *(makes 8 servings)*

- ♥ 8 ounces Korean style of starch noodle
- ♥ 1 cup shredded carrot
- ♥ 1 cup shredded celery
- ♥ 2 tablespoons soy sauce
- ♥ 2 tablespoons sesame oil
- ♥ 1 tablespoon hot sauce
- ♥ Pinch of salt and sugar

胡蘿蔔和芹菜沙拉

Cooking Steps:

1. Break starch noodle in half and drop them in boiling water. Cook for 12 minutes until soft.

2. Rinse with cold water and drain. Put cooked noodle in a large bowl.

3. Cut celery into 2-inch long thin strips, soak with a little bit salt for 20 minutes, then rinse with cold water and squeeze dry. Add it to the noodle.

4. Julienne carrot into 2-inch long, soak with a little bit salt for 20 minutes, rinse and squeeze dry. Add to the noodle bowl.

5. In a small mixing bowl, combine and mix soy sauce, sugar, sesame oil and hot sauce, for the seasoning sauce. Pour the sauce onto the noodle and vegetables, mix well. Taste for seasoning.

6. Tip: this is a great vegetarian dish, you can substitute these vegetables with your favorite ones.

Shredded Turnips and Jellyfish Salad

Ingredients: *(makes 8 to 10 servings)*

- ♥ 1 package of jellyfish (whole)
- ♥ 2 medium size turnips, shredded
- ♥ 4 stalks green onions, finely diced
- ♥ 1 tablespoon salt
- ♥ 3 tablespoons vegetable oil

涼拌蘿蔔絲海蜇皮

Cooking Steps:

1. Shred turnips, add salt and soak for two hours, leave it in refrigerator; soak overnight will have a better flavor.

2. Squeeze shredded turnips dry and put into a big bowl, ready to use.

3. Rinse jellyfish and wash out all sea salt. Soak jellyfish in cold water for a few hours to reduce the fishy smell. It may take up to four hours, or do it over night.

4. Rinse jellyfish again before use. Shred jellyfish and squeeze out the water, or you leave them in a colander to drain the access water.

5. Spread shredded jellyfish over the turnips.

6. Spread the diced green onion over the jellyfish and form a three-layer salad.

7. Heat the cooking oil in the sauce pan with high heat for 30 seconds, pour the hot oil over the salad, listen to the sizzling sound. If you did not heard the sizzling sound, that means the oil is not hot enough. You can take the green onions (the top layer of salad) back to the sauce pan, quickly stir and continue to sizzle. Then, mix with other ingredients thoroughly, taste for seasoning.

8. Transfer to a plate. Serve it cold.

9. This dish is good for all seasons. In summer, you can keep it in refrigerator for few days, and for up to a week in winter season.

Veggie Goose

Ingredients: *(makes 6 to 8 servings)*

- ♥ 2 tablespoons vegetable oil
- ♥ 1 cup shitake mushrooms, soaked and drain
- ♥ 3/4 cup bamboo shoot, shreds
- ♥ 1 tablespoon soy sauce
- ♥ 1/2 teaspoon brown sugar
- ♥ 2 tablespoons white wine
- ♥ 1/2 cup water
- ♥ 2 pounds fresh bean curd folded sheets (so called FU TZU)

Note: buy the folded fresh bean curd skins. If you can't find them, use the big round one but need different cooking steps to make, which is not given here.

Cooking Steps:

For Filling:

1. Heat oil in a medium pan, over medium-high heat, add mushrooms and bamboo shoots, stir about 2 minutes. Add soy sauce and water, stir another minute.

2. Add wine, cover and cook for 5 to 7 minutes more until juice is evaporated. Remove from heat, let it cool.

For Veggie Goose:

1. Butterfly each fresh FUTZU, place the filling evenly on one side and close it, finish all veggie geese; set aside.

2. Heat oil in same pan over medium heat, lay down the veggie geese. Pan fry each side a couple minutes until lightly golden brown.

3. Add soy sauce, brown sugar, water and wine, make sure that the liquid covers all veggie geese.

4. Cook for 10 minutes with medium-low heat until the juice is evaporated. The skin should be soft and tender; if not, add more water and cook another 5 minutes.

5. Slice and serve either in warm or cold.

6. This is a very popular vegetarian cold plate in any seasons. The leftovers can be frozen up to one month.

Braised Pork Shoulder

Ingredients: *(makes 6 to 8 servings)*

- ♥ 3 to 4 pounds pork shoulder
- ♥ 3 tablespoons dry sherry or cooking wine
- ♥ 3 stalks scallions, cut lengthwise
- ♥ 3 pieces sliced ginger
- ♥ 3 cloves star anise
- ♥ 5 tablespoons dark soy sauce
- ♥ 4 tablespoons crushed rock sugar
- ♥ 1 tablespoon salt
- ♥ 1/2 pound baby green veggies for garnish
- ♥ cooking oil

紅燒豬蹄膀

Cooking Steps:

1. Clean pork shoulder with tap water and remove any hair off the skin, pat dry.

2. Rub pork shoulder with salt, up, down and all over. Let it sit a while.

3. Coat a large sauté pan with cooking oil and bring to a medium heat, pan fry the pork shoulder, each side, until skin is crisp and brown. Remove the pork shoulder from the pan and discard the excess oil.

4. Heat 1 tablespoon oil in the same pan, stir-fry ginger, scallions, star anise and sugar, cook a few minutes until the flavor are combined.

5. Return pork shoulder to the pan, add wine, soy sauce, and cook a few minutes. Pour water to 2/3 the way of pork shoulder, covered and bring it to boil. Turn the heat to simmer and continue to cook for 1 1/2 to 2 hours or until the meat are tender soft and almost falling off the bone. Check it periodically to make sure the liquid isn't dry-up and the skin is not sticking to the bottom of the pot.

6. At the end, increase the heat and boil to reduce the sauce for a few minutes, or until they are thick and glossy.

7. Meanwhile, blanch green vegetables in boiling water for one minute. Plunge into cold water immediately. Drain and dry; lightly dust with salt.

8. Arrange greens along the outside layer of a serving plate as a ring, for garnish. Transfer the pork shoulder to the center of the plate, pour a couple of tablespoons of meat sauce on top, slice and serve.

Chinese New Year Tuan-Yuan Hot Pot

Ingredients: *(makes 8 to 10 servings)*

- 12 ounces fresh fish (salmon or Cod)
- 12 ounces medium to large shrimp
- 6 ounces ham or prosciutto
- 2 fresh bamboo shoots, sliced
- 6 fresh or dry mushrooms, sliced
- 15 to 20 pieces of snow peas
- 2 tablespoons chopped scallions
- 1 ginger, sliced
- 4 ounces dried cellophane noodles, soaked
- 1 Napa cabbage, sliced and boiled
- 1 (14-ounce) can of chicken soup
- 12 golden nuggets 'Dan-Jiao' (recipe follows)
- 12 meatballs (recipe follows) or fish balls

Note: you may use other ingredients to assemble the hot pot as long as the food colors are contrasting.

Need an electric skillet.

Cooking Steps:

Assemble New Year's 'Tuan Yuan' Hot Pot

1. Slice fish into one inch wide by three inches long and a quarter of inch thick fillet. Marinate fish fillets with 1/4 teaspoon salt and 1 teaspoon cooking wine for 30 minutes.

2. Chop cabbage into long strands, place them in a big pot; add a cup water, cook for 3 minutes. Drain and set aside.

3. Soak the cellophane noodles in warm tap water for 5 minutes. Drain and set aside. (the first 3 steps can be done a day ahead)

4. Lay all ingredients in the hot pot attractively. The beauty of this dish is the color. When using green veggies like snow peas, choose white or beige color like bamboo shoots for contrast. Adding red color ingredients, like shrimp or ham is recommended because of New Year celebration. The final hot pot assembled should have layers of round circles as a symbol of 'tuan yuan'.

5. Recommended layer of arrangement:

   First layer- bottom of the electric skillet

   ♦ Lay down sliced cabbage over the bottom of the electric pan

   ♦ Add clear noodle in between the cabbage

   ♦ Spread all mushrooms over the cabbage and noodle

   ♦ Drop a few pieces of ginger root

Chinese New Year
Tuan-Yuan Hot Pot

Cooking Steps: (continue)

Second layer- starting from the center toward the outer wall of the electric skillet

♦ Place the meat balls in the center of the hot pot

♦ Lay the fish fillet (horizontal direction) next to meat balls on both sides. Place down dan-jiao next to fish fillet and form a half moon shape. Arrange bamboo shoots and sugar peas next to dan-jiao

Third layer

♦ Place shrimp as a divider (vertical direction) in between the ingredients on 2nd layer (It can form 5 new-moon shaped columns).

♦ Lay the meat, prosciutto or ham, along the outer wall to form a circle.

Add chicken broth and two cups of water into the pot and bring to boil. Continue to cook until all ingredients are cooked, about 10 minutes. Season to taste. Sprinkle some chopped scallion. Serve immediately.

Golden Nuggets ("DAN-JIAO") and Meatballs

- ♥ 1 pound ground pork
- ♥ 6 eggs plus one egg white
- ♥ 2 tablespoons minced scallion
- ♥ 1 teaspoon minced ginger
- ♥ 1 tablespoon cooking wine

Cooking Steps:

1. Combine pork with egg white, cooking wine, green onions, ginger, soy sauce, and salt. Mix them thoroughly, set aside. Beat 6 eggs with pinch of salt.

2. Heat 1 tablespoon oil in the sauce pan; lightly coat the pan with oil. Turn the heat to medium-low.

3. Remove excess oil to a small bowl, save it for re-oiling the pan before pouring the egg mixture.

4. Pour 2 tablespoons of egg mixture into the center of the pan to form a small egg pancake.

5. Place a teaspoon of meat mixture at the center of egg pancake, carefully fold one side of egg pancake over and form a half moon shape which symbolizes a 'Yuan-Bau'(元寶). Flip over after 30 seconds or until the egg is cooked. Transfer dan-jiao to a plate.

6. Repeat steps 4 through 8 to finish up all egg mixture, makes approximately 2 dozens of dan-jiao.

7. To make the meatballs: place about 1 tablespoon of meat mixture and roll it around in your moistened hand to shape it into a ball-sized meatball. Finish making about 20 meatballs.

8. Steam dan-giao and meatballs in a steamer or a rice cooker for 20 minutes.

9. Dan-Jiao and meatballs can be prepared days ahead.

Cod Fillet Rolls
in Sweet and Sour Sauce

Ingredients: (makes 8 servings)

- ♥ 2 to 21/2 pounds fresh cod fillet
- ♥ 2 ounces ham, sliced thin
- ♥ 1 ginger, shredded
- ♥ 2 scallions, shredded
- ♥ 2 cups flour
- ♥ 2 cups bread crumb
- ♥ 2 eggs, beat with 1 tablespoon water
- ♥ 2 cloves garlic, chopped
- ♥ 1 shallot, chopped
- ♥ 1 jalapeño, thinly sliced
- ♥ 1/2 cup shredded carrot
- ♥ 1/2 cup shredded celery
- ♥ Vegetable oil

Preheat oven to 325 degrees F

Cooking Steps:

1. Rinse cod fillets and pat dry. Cut fish crosswise into 31/2" x 2" x 1/3". Marinate fish with 1 tsp salt and 1/2 cup white wine for 15 minutes. Prepare three separate shallow dishes, for flour, egg wash and bread crumb.

2. Prepare for sweet and sour sauce: in a small bowl, mix well 2 tsp hot bean paste, 2 tbsp dry sherry wine, 1 tsp sesame oil, 3 tbsp ketchup, 3 tbsp rice vinegar and 3 tbsp brown sugar; set aside. Dissolve 2 tbsp corn starch with water; set aside

3. Lay the fish fillet on a flat surface, put a slice of ham, a few pieces of ginger and scallions in the center then roll up, brush a little bit corn starch to close up. Dip fish roll in flour, then egg wash, finally coat with bread crumb. Repeat all fish rolls, set aside.

4. Heat the oil in a sauté pan with medium high heat. Place fish rolls evenly and leave room between rolls. Cook 2 minutes on one side then flip it over and cook again for 1 minute or until the crust coating is brown. Transfer fish rolls into a baking pan.

5. Bake for 5 minutes or until fish is cooked. Transfer fish rolls to a plate.

6. Heat the oil in the sauté pan. Add the scallions, ginger, shallots and garlic and stir-fry until aromatic (about 30 seconds). Add the carrots and celeries, stir-fry for another minute.

7. Add the sweet and sour sauce and bring it to a boil; add corn starch water, stir to thicken. Season to taste. Pour the sauce over; make sure each roll is coated with sauce. Serve immediately.

Diced Chicken
with Assorted Peppers

Ingredients: *(makes 6 servings)*

- ♥ 1 pound boneless and skinless chicken breast
- ♥ 1 each green, red and yellow peppers
- ♥ 1 cup water chestnut
- ♥ 1 teaspoon grated ginger
- ♥ 2 stalks green onions, chopped
- ♥ 1 teaspoon minced garlic
- ♥ 1 jalapeño, sliced

Marinade:

- ♥ 1 tablespoon light soy sauce
- ♥ 1 tablespoon white wine
- ♥ 1/2 teaspoon salt
- ♥ 1 egg white
- ♥ 2 tablespoons cornstarch

辣子雞丁

Cooking Steps:

1. Cut chicken breast into 1/2-inch cubes. Mix together with marinade sauce.

2. Dice all peppers, water chestnuts into cubes, same size as chicken.

3. Prepare the seasoning sauce: in a small bowl, combine and mix well with 1 tbsp soy sauce, 1 tbsp red vinegar, 1/2 tsp white wine, 1/2 tsp brown sugar, 1/2 tsp salt, 1 tsp sesame oil, 1 tbsp hot bean paste sauce, and 1 tsp chopped scallion. Set aside. Mix 1 tsp cornstarch with water. Ready to use.

4. Heat 2 tablespoon of oil, stir-fry jalapeño over high heat for about 30 seconds. Add in chicken, cook for one minute or until the color changes. Remove chicken.

5. Heat oil, stir-fry green onions, ginger and garlic for a minute or two. Add in all vegetables and cook it another minute.

6. Return chicken to the pan, add seasoning sauce, stir and mix it thoroughly. Thicken the sauce with cornstarch water, if needed.

7. Turn off the heat and sprinkle with chopped green onions. Taste and serve.

Ground Meat Bean Curd Rolls

Ingredients: *(makes 6 to 8 servings)*

- ♥ 1 pound ground turkey or ground pork
- ♥ 1 6-ounce package of <u>dried</u> bean curd sheets
- ♥ 1 ben-jan (dried bamboo shoot) or 3 shiitake mushrooms
- ♥ Two (15-inch) strings

Marinade:

- ♥ 1 egg white
- ♥ 1 tablespoon soy sauce
- ♥ 1 tablespoon white wine
- ♥ 3 stalks green onions, chopped
- ♥ 1/2 teaspoon grated ginger
- ♥ Pinch of salt

腐皮肉卷

Cooking Steps:

1. Marinate ground meat with marinade sauce for 30 minutes.

2. The dried bamboo shoot named ben-jan means the tip of the bamboo shoot. It needs to soak in warm water for 5 minutes and to rinse off the salty flavor. Cut ben-jan into thin pieces. You may substitute it with three shiitake mushrooms, if ben-jan is not available.

3. Soak dried bean curd sheets in kitchen sink with luke-warm water for a few minutes. Drain and place them between damp towels, ready to use.

4. For each soaked bean curd sheet, cut into three to four equal size squares (approx.).

5. Put a tablespoon of meat filling in center of the square; roll it like to make a spring roll. Lay it at the bottom of a cooking container.

6. Continue the process; stack up them into two bundles. Tie each bundle of meat rolls with a string to avoid them moving around, while it cooks.

7. Add the bamboo shoot or mushrooms in, season with 1 tablespoon soy sauce and pinch of salt. Pour a cup of water over; water should be at or below the meat rolls.

8. Steam meat rolls on the stove with high heat or cook it in a rice cooker for 25 to 30 minutes.

9. Transfer meat rolls to a serving bowl; pour the meat juice over and serve it immediately.

10. This dish is a favorite dish for all age groups.

Kung Pao Chicken

Ingredients: (*makes 6 to 8 servings*)

- 2 boneless, skinless chicken breasts
- 2 small jalapeños
- 4 red dry peppers, add more if you desire
- 1/2 cup roasted unsalted peanuts
- 2 tablespoons shallots
- 1 teaspoon finely minced ginger
- 1 clove garlic, minced
- 1 teaspoon chopped scallion
- 1 package of soft tortillas (optional)
- Salt and pepper

Marinade:
- 1 tablespoon dark soy sauce
- 1 tablespoon sherry or white wine
- 1 teaspoon cornstarch
- Dash of salt

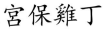

宮保雞丁

Cooking Steps:

1. Cut chicken breasts into 3/4-inch cubes. Marinate with soy sauce, white wine and cornstarch for 20 minutes.

2. Dice jalapeños into small cubes.

3. Prepare the hot bean sauce: in a small bowl, combine and mix well 1 tsp hot bean paste sauce, 1 tsp red vinegar, 1 tbsp white wine, 1 tsp brown sugar, 1/2 tsp salt, 1/2 tsp sesame oil, 1 tsp chopped scallion and 1 tsp cornstarch with water. Ready to use.

4. Heat 1 tablespoon of oil, stir-fry dry red peppers, jalapeño and shallots over high heat for a few seconds. Add garlic, ginger and chicken, cook for two minutes. Then add a tablespoon sherry, 1 tsp brown sugar and a dash of salt continue to cook or until chicken is tender.

5. Pour in hot bean sauce mixture and cook for another minute. Taste for seasoning.

6. Turn off the heat, stir in roasted peanuts. Sprinkle chopped scallion.

7. Serve with rice or warm tortillas wraps.

Lion's Head Meatballs

Ingredients: *(makes 8 servings)*

- 2 pounds ground pork
- 3 1/2 pounds Napa cabbage
- 8 pieces sliced ginger
- 2 tablespoons soy sauce
- 1 1/2 slices white bread, trim off the crust
- 2 tablespoons white wine or rice wine, divided
- 3 tablespoons cornstarch, divided

Marinade:

- 2 stalks green onions, finely chopped
- 1 tablespoon grated ginger
- 2 tablespoons white wine
- 1 teaspoon cornstarch
- 1 tablespoon soy sauce
- 1/2 teaspoon sesame oil
- 1 egg
- 1/4 cup water
- Salt

Cooking Steps:

1. Cut each cabbage in half, and then cut each half into 3 or 4 pieces, lengthwise. Rinse and remove the hard stand. Cook them in a big pot with half cup water at low to medium heat, until tender, about 10 to 15 minutes. Turn off heat.

2. Soak bread with water, quickly remove and squeeze off the water.

3. In a large mixing bowl, mix ground pork with egg, wine, soy sauce, green onion, ginger, sesame oil, cornstarch, salt, water and soaked bread. Stir them in <u>one</u> direction for 3 to 5 minutes or until they are well mixed. Divide it into 8 to10 equal portions, or your favor size of the meatballs.

4. In a small bowl, mix 2 tablespoons cornstarch with water, soy sauce and cooking wine; set aside.

5. Add cooking oil in a cast iron or skillet pan with medium-high heat. To form a meatball, working with both hands. Place a portion of meat on your moistened left hand; on your right hand, take a spoon slightly coat with cornstarch mixture and then use it and the left palm to shape it into a meatball.

6. Cook meat balls in batches, pan fry until both sides are browned, about 10 minutes.

7. Transfer meatballs to a plate. Deglaze the pan with wine, cook a minute. Load in vegetables with its broth, then place meatballs on the top; add soy sauce and ginger pieces, cover and cook in medium heat for 25 minutes or the meat starts tender and soft. Turn heat to low, simmer for another 15 minutes or until the meatballs are cooked through.

8. Season to taste, serve immediately.

Ma-Po (Spicy) Tofu

Ingredients: *(makes 6 to 8 servings)*

- ♥ 1/2 pound ground turkey
- ♥ 1 to 2 packages soft or silken tofu
- ♥ 1 cup of chicken broth
- ♥ 1 teaspoon sesame oil
- ♥ 2 stalks green onions, chopped
- ♥ 1 teaspoon grated fresh ginger
- ♥ 3 cloves garlic, minced
- ♥ 2 teaspoons shallots, minced
- ♥ 1 tablespoon white wine
- ♥ 1 tablespoon soy sauce
- ♥ 1 tablespoon hot bean paste or hot sauce
- ♥ Salt
- ♥ 1 tablespoon cornstarch with some water
- ♥ Cooking oil for sautéing

麻婆豆腐

Cooking Steps:

1. Open tofu package, gently rinse tofu with cold tap water. Cut them into 3/4-inch cubes.

2. Sauté shallots, green onions, minced garlic, and grated ginger in a sauce pan over high heat for a minute or two. Add ground turkey, sauté until tender and brown; then add hot bean paste, mix them well. Pour white wine and chicken stock, cook a few more minutes.

3. Bring tofu into the meat sauce, season with soy sauce, cook thoroughly or until all flavors are combined.

4. Thicken with cornstarch water, taste for seasoning.

5. Turn off the heat, sprinkle chopped green onions and sesame oil. Serve immediately.

Minced Shrimp in Lettuce Wrap

Ingredients: *(makes 8 to 10 servings)*

- ♥ 1 pound medium shrimp
- ♥ 8 ounces ground pork
- ♥ 1 stalk king oyster mushrooms, diced
- ♥ 1 medium size fresh bamboo shoot, diced
- ♥ 6 water chestnuts diced
- ♥ 1 yellow pepper, diced
- ♥ 1 stalk celery, diced
- ♥ 1 jalapeño, seeded and diced
- ♥ 3 cloves garlic, minced
- ♥ 1 teaspoon grated ginger
- ♥ 2 teaspoons shallots, diced
- ♥ 1 tablespoon white wine or cooking wine
- ♥ 12 pieces lettuce
- ♥ 2 ounces pine nuts

Cooking Steps:

1. Peel, devein and clean the shrimp, dice them into small pieces, marinate with 1 tbsp white wine and 1 tsp corn starch.

2. Marinate ground pork with 1 tbsp soy sauce for minimum 20 minutes

3. Toast pine nuts in oven (at 275°F) for 15 minutes.

4. Place oil in a large sauce pan over high heat. Sauté shallot for 30 seconds, add mushrooms, bamboo shoots and stir for a minute, then mix with rest vegetables, and cook for another minute or so. Transfer them to a plate.

5. Heat oil in the same pan, sauté jalapeño, garlic, and ginger for 30 seconds, add ground pork, stir-fry a minute. Transfer them to a plate.

6. Next, heat oil, sauté green onion and ginger for 30 seconds, add shrimp, cook for a minute, add cooking wine and mix well.

7. Bring all cooked vegetables back to sauce pan, season with 1 tsp soy sauce, 1/2 tsp brown sugar and 1/2 tsp sesame oil; stir thoroughly and thicken the sauce with 1 tbsp cornstarch and water, if needed. Cook a few more minutes, or until all food flavors are combined, taste for seasoning. Turn off the heat, sprinkle pine nuts and sesame oil.

8. Serve this dish in chilled lettuce wrap. You may add more pine nuts on each individual lettuce wrap before serving.

9. Tip: for this dish, it is not necessary to use all listed vegetables in the recipe, you can just use any two, in addition to shrimp and meat.

Sauté Prawn with Tomato Sauce

Ingredients: *(makes 8 to 10 servings)*

- 1 1/2 to 2 pounds large size prawn
- 3 stalks green onions, chopped
- 3 tablespoons minced ginger
- 2 tablespoons minced garlic
- 1 teaspoon shallot
- 1 small jalapeño
- 2 teaspoons ketchup
- 2 tablespoons hot bean sauce
- 2 tablespoons white wine
- 1/2 cup corn starch
- 1 1/2 tablespoons brown sugar
- 2/3 cup water
- Salt

乾燒明蝦

Cooking Steps:

1. Cut off the antennae and other appendages from the prawns, and devein, rinse them thoroughly; cut each prawn along the vein to one-third deep but not cut through, for about an inch long. Drain them and dry.

2. Put corn starch in a flat shallow dish; coat the prawns with corn starch just before cooking.

3. Place oil in a large sauce pan over high heat. Sauté prawns for 2 minutes or until each prawn curled and turn red. Transfer them to a plate.

4. Heat oil in the same pan, sauté jalapeño, green onion, ginger, garlic for a minute, add ketchup, hot bean paste, brown sugar and wine, cook for a minute or two. Add prawns back to the sauce. Add fresh home-made tomato sauce and thicken with cornstarch and water, bring to boil or until all food flavors are married.

5. Taste for seasoning. Serve immediately.

Homemade tomato sauce:

1. Cut three large tomatoes in small cubes.

2. Cook tomatoes in a small sauté pan for a few minutes, add 1 teaspoon minced ginger, 1 teaspoon minced shallot and 1 tablespoon brown sugar continue cook until the juice/water level is complete evaporated, about 45 minutes.

3. Taste for seasoning.

Paper-Wrapped Chicken

Ingredients: (makes 12 to 24 servings)

- ♥ 2 pounds chicken breast or chicken thigh or mixed
- ♥ 5 stalks scallions
- ♥ 6 dried black mushrooms, soaked
- ♥ 1/2 pound fresh mushrooms, sliced
- ♥ 4 ounces ham
- ♥ 8 pieces red, orange and yellow (small) peppers
- ♥ 1 bunch cilantro
- ♥ Aluminum foil sheet, 6-inch squares or larger
- ♥ Vegetable oil for deep fry

Marinade:

- ♥ 1 teaspoon sugar
- ♥ 1/2 teaspoon finely chopped ginger
- ♥ 1 tablespoon barbecue sauce (Bull Head brand)
- ♥ 3 tablespoons soy sauce
- ♥ 1 tablespoon sesame oil
- ♥ 2 tablespoons white wine
- ♥ Pinch of salt and pepper

紙包雞

Cooking Steps:

1. Cut chicken breast into thin slices roughly 1-inch x 3-inch shape. Marinate the chicken with marinade sauce, cover and refrigerate for 45 minutes or overnight.

2. Cut soaked and fresh mushrooms in thin pieces, sauté them with white wine and salt for five minutes.

3. Cut small peppers thinly. Cut ham into 1-inch x 2-inch shape. Cut green onions into 1-inch long. Put them in separate containers.

4. Take one aluminum foil; brush the center with cooking oil or sesame oil. Place chicken, ham, mushrooms, peppers, green onion and cilantro in the middle of aluminum foil. Usually the cook method will determine how much ingredients to wrap, e.g. the small wrap for quick deep-frying and large size wrap for bake or steam.

5. To wrap, fold the foil over to form a triangle, then fold right side over towards the center, followed by fold left side over, then roll it tight like to make a spring roll or roll and fold like a parcel (large wrap).

6. There are three ways to cook:
   - to deep fry, stir occasionally until the chicken is cooked through, about 6 minutes. Drain on paper towels, cook in batches.
   - to steam for 25 minutes;
   - to bake in oven (at 350°F) for 22 to 25 minutes.

7. Serve paper-wrapped chicken on a large plate, garnished with green veggies.

8. Tip: you can substitute chicken with salmon fillets, wrap in large size and bake for 25 minutes.

Sautéed Mixed Vegetables

Ingredients: (makes 8 to 10 servings)

- 3 pieces dry bean curd
- 2 ounces dried black fungus, soaked
- 2 ounces dried lily, soaked
- 6 ounces dried bean curd sticks, soaked
- 3 ounces dried shiitake mushrooms, soaked
- 1 fresh bamboo shoot, sliced
- 8 pieces fresh water chestnuts, skinned and sliced
- 3 ounces pea pod
- 2 carrots, sliced
- 1 can fried gluten, drained and washed
- 3 ounces soy bean peas
- 1 tablespoon white wine
- 1 tablespoon brown sugar
- 1/2 teaspoon sesame oil
- 2 tablespoons soy sauce
- Pure olive oil or cooking oil

炒素

Cooking Steps:

1. Soak dry ingredients in hot or boiling water, rinse it thoroughly. This can be done days ahead. Slice all ingredients in large pieces. Cut soaked dry lily in half.

2. Place oil in a large sauce pan over high heat. Sauté soy bean peas for a minute then add in carrots and green pea pods, stir for a few minutes. Taste for seasoning, transfer them to a plate.

3. Heat oil in the same pan, sauté mushrooms, bamboo shoots and water chestnuts, add cooking wine, cook for a minute or two. Taste for seasoning, transfer them to a plate.

4. Heat 1 tablespoon of oil, sauté black fungus first, then add the rest of vegetables, lily flower, bean curd, bean curd sticks and fried gluten. Add seasoning and cook for few more minutes.

5. Return cooked mushrooms, bamboo shoots, etc. back to the sauce pan, except for the green veggies. Season with soy sauce, brown sugar and 1 cup of water. Turn heat to medium low and continue to cook for 15 minutes, heat them thoroughly or until all food flavors are married.

6. Bring back the greens, pea pods and soybean peas, add sesame oil, and taste for seasoning.

7. Serve warm or cold.

8. Tip: this great vegetarian dish serves all seasons; to choose many colorful fresh or dried vegetables would give this dish more pleasure.

Shredded Pork Tenderloin And Green Bean Sheet Delight

Ingredients: *(makes 6 to 8 servings)*

- ♥ 1 package Tian Jin green beans sheets
- ♥ 1/2 pound pork tenderloin, thinly shredded
- ♥ 5 green onions, thinly shredded
- ♥ 1 English cucumber, thinly shredded
- ♥ 2 jalapeños, thinly sliced
- ♥ 2 tablespoons white wine
- ♥ 1 tablespoon soy sauce
- ♥ Pinch of salt

肉絲粉皮

Cooking Steps:

1. Shred pork tenderloin; marinate pork with salt, wine and soy sauce for 30 minutes.

2. Cut English cucumber diagonally into thin slices; spread them evenly at the bottom of the plate. This is the first layer.

3. Bring a pot of water to boil, drop three or four pieces bean sheets to boil. Cook for 10 to 15 minutes or until soft and clear. Rinse with cold water and drain well.

4. Cut bean sheets into desired shape and size, transfer them to the plate and spread over the shredded cucumbers. This is the second layer.

5. Heat oil in a sauté pan; stir-fry jalapeños for a couple of minutes. Add shredded pork and stir until meat is tender. Stir in green onion and add more wine or water if the juice dried up; taste for seasoning.

6. Place meat and green onion over bean sheets to form a three-layer delighted green bean sheet dish.

7. Toss well just before serving.

Steam Pearl Balls

Ingredients: *(makes 8 to 10 servings)*

- ♥ 1 pound medium-size shrimp
- ♥ 8 ounces ground pork
- ♥ 1 cup sweet rice
- ♥ 1 tablespoon white wine
- ♥ 1 tablespoon finely grated ginger
- ♥ 3 stalks green onions, chopped
- ♥ 1 egg
- ♥ 2 teaspoons soy sauce
- ♥ 1 teaspoon water
- ♥ 2 teaspoons cornstarch
- ♥ 1 carrot, thin diced in small pieces (optional)
- ♥ Salt

珍珠丸子

Cooking Steps:

1. Soak sweet rice about an hour, drain well and keep in refrigerator. It can be done a few hours ahead.

2. Peel, devein and clean the shrimp, dice them into small pieces, keep in refrigerator. Coat with 1 t. corn-starch just before use.

3. Mix shrimp meat with ground pork, marinate with soy sauce, white wine, egg, ginger, and green onion, keep it in refrigerator.

4. Spread rice on a flat plate (dash with a little cornstarch if you wish).

5. Mix the remaining cornstarch with water in a small bowl and set aside.

6. Wet a tablespoon with cornstarch water; fill a spoonful of shrimp and pork mixture into a ball by using your palm to help.

7. Make one pearl ball at a time and roll it over the sweet rice; make sure it coats with rice completely.

8. Place pearl balls in the steamer on a damp cheesecloth, arrange them with a little space in between. Decorate it with a piece of carrot on top.

9. Steam pearl balls for about 12 minutes over high heat.

10. Serve immediately.

Steam Whole Fish
in Microwave Oven

Ingredients: *(makes 4 servings)*

- ♥ 2 1-pound whole fresh fish, rainbow trout, black bass or strip bass
- ♥ 2 tablespoons shredded ginger
- ♥ 3 stalks scallions, thinly sliced in 2-inch long
- ♥ 1/2 cup medium-dry sherry or rice wine
- ♥ 2 tablespoons soy sauce
- ♥ Pinch of salt
- ♥ Cooking oil

Cooking Steps:

1. Clean fish with tap cold water, dry it with paper towel. Make two or three slashes, diagonally, on each side of fish, lightly sprinkle with salt. Let it stand for 5 minutes.

2. Lightly coat with cooking oil on an oven-proof dish, large enough to hold the whole fish. Lay fish on it. Pour half the wine over and place dish in microwave oven.

3. Cover and cook on high heat for 5 to 7 minutes, or until fish is fully cooked, remove.

4. Spread shredded ginger and green onions on top of the fish then pour soy sauce over and add more wine.

5. Meanwhile, heat 2 tablespoons oil in a sauté pan on high heat. When the oil is heated, pour it over immediately to sizzle the scallion and ginger on top. If the oil is not hot enough or you didn't hear the sizzling sound, return the scallion and ginger along with the (fish) juice to sauté pan, quickly stir a few more seconds then pour it over the fish.

6. Serve immediately.

Stir-Fried Assorted Vegetables

Ingredients: *(makes 10 servings)*

- ♥ 4 pieces dry bean curd
- ♥ 3 ounces shiitake mushrooms
- ♥ 2 stalks king oyster mushrooms
- ♥ 1 medium sized fresh bamboo shoot
- ♥ 1 Szechuan preserved vegetable
- ♥ 3 ounces pea pod
- ♥ 2 carrots
- ♥ 2 celery stalks
- ♥ 1 large jalapeño, seeded and shredded
- ♥ 3 ounces bean sprout
- ♥ 2 shallots, shredded
- ♥ 1 tablespoon white wine
- ♥ 1 tablespoon soy sauce
- ♥ Pinch of salt and brown sugar
- ♥ 1 teaspoon sesame oil
- ♥ Pure olive oil or any cooking oil

Cooking Steps:

1. Soak shiitake mushrooms in the boiling water, drain well and shred.

2. Rinse Szechuan preserved vegetable in tap water to reduce the salty flavor, drain well and shred.

3. Cut or shred all vegetables, bean curd, bamboo shoot, carrots, celery, etc. in thin strips at same size and length. Set aside.

4. Place oil in a large sauce pan over high heat. Sauté shallots and jalapeño (half) for 30 seconds, add bean curd and stir for few minutes, then add in Szechuan preserved vegetables, and cook for another 2 minutes. Transfer to a plate.

5. Heat oil in the same pan, sauté mushrooms and bamboo shoots, add cooking wine, and stir well. Taste for seasoning, transfer them to the plate.

6. Heat oil again, sauté the remaining jalapeño for few seconds, drop carrots, celery and pea pods; stir for a couple of minutes. Season with salt and heat them thoroughly.

7. Bring all cooked vegetables back to sauce pan, add bean sprout at last. Season with soy sauce, brown sugar and sesame oil; stir thoroughly. Cook a few more minutes, or until all food flavors are combined. Taste for seasoning.

8. Serve warm.

9. This great vegetarian dish (十全十美) serves perfectly on the Chinese New Year Eve.

Stir-Fried Beef with Asparagus

Ingredients: *(makes 6 to 8 servings)*

- ♥ 1 pound beef flank steak
- ♥ 3 stalks scallions, cut 1" long
- ♥ 1 ginger, sliced
- ♥ 11/2 pounds asparagus
- ♥ 1 shallot, finely chopped
- ♥ 1 jalapeño, thinly sliced

Marinade:

- ♥ 1 teaspoon salt
- ♥ 1 tablespoon soy sauce
- ♥ 1 tablespoon vegetable oil
- ♥ 1 tablespoon white wine
- ♥ 1 teaspoon cornstarch with water

蘆筍炒牛肉

Cooking Steps:

1. Cut beef crosswise into 1-inch x 2-inch slices; marinate beef for 25 minutes.

2. For seasoning sauce, in a small bowl, mix well 1 tbsp soy sauce, 1 tbsp hot bean paste, 2 tbsp dry sherry, 1 tsp sesame oil, 1 tsp orange juice, 1 tsp brown sugar, and 2 tsp corn starch with water; set aside.

3. Clean asparagus and peel the skin, trim off the tough ends. Place asparagus in boiling water and blanch for 1 minute. Then remove and toss them into the ice cold water; drain and dry.

4. Heat oil in a sauté pan with high heat. Stir-fry jalapeño for 30 seconds, add beef and continue stirring for 30 seconds or until beef is medium rare. Transfer beef into a plate.

5. Heat oil in the sauté pan, stir-fry the shallots for few seconds; add green onions, and ginger, stir until aromatic (about 30 seconds). Add beef and cook for 20 seconds.

6. Add asparagus, pour seasoning sauce over, quickly stir in high heat to thicken the sauce. Season to taste, serve immediately.

7. You may substitute asparagus with other greens, like broccoli, green pepper or snow peas.

Veggie Yellow Birds

Ingredients: *(makes 12 servings)*

- ♥ 1 package of <u>fresh</u> bean curd sheets (whole round shape sheets in the freezer section)
- ♥ 1 large carrot, shredded
- ♥ 1 cup bean sprouts
- ♥ 1 cup soaked black fungus (wood ears), shredded
- ♥ 1 tablespoon soy sauce (divided)
- ♥ 1 teaspoon brown sugar
- ♥ 1/2 teaspoon sesame oil
- ♥ Salt
- ♥ 1/2 cup water
- ♥ 1 bag of any vegetables like spinach, bok choy, broccoli or pea sprouts.

Cooking Steps:

1. Blanch bean sprouts in boiling water for 30 seconds.

2. In a sauce pan, stir-fry carrots, black fungus for two minutes, add bean sprouts and season with salt and soy sauce, mix them well. Transfer it to a plate, let it cool.

3. Take 2 round bean curd sheets out of the package. Cut each sheet into 6 equal size triangles.

4. Soak 3 to 4 triangle sheets a time in lukewarm water for a few seconds and place them between damp towels. Sock a few sheets a time to avoid them break up before use.

5. Take one triangle sheet on a chopping board or a flat surface, place a spoonful of filling towards to the tip; roll it up gently. Tie a knot at the end; it should look like a bird.

6. Continue the process, you'll make a total of 12 veggie birds.

7. Heat the cooking oil in the sauce pan with medium heat, pan fry the birds for 60 seconds or until golden brown. Flip over and cook for another minute or so.

8. Season with soy sauce, brown sugar, salt, sesame oil, and water; cover and cook for 5 minutes or until the water is evaporated. Taste for seasoning.

9. Sauté green vegetables for a few minutes, season with a little garlic and salt. Transfer it to a serving plate to make a bird nest.

10. Lay the yellow birds onto the nest. Serve it immediately.

11. This great vegetarian dish serves good for all seasons.

Wuxi Style Pork Ribs

Ingredients: *(makes 6 to 8 servings)*

- ♥ 21/2 pounds pork baby back ribs, cut into ribs
- ♥ 3 stalks green onions, cut into long pieces
- ♥ 1 ginger, sliced
- ♥ 4 tablespoons ketchup
- ♥ 1/2 teaspoon salt
- ♥ 1/2 cup dark soy sauce, divided
- ♥ 1/2 cup light soy sauce, divided
- ♥ 4 pieces star anise (whole)
- ♥ 1/2 cup white wine
- ♥ 11/2 tablespoons yellow rock sugar

無錫排骨

Cooking Steps:

1. Season pork ribs with salt, 1/4 cup light and 1/4 cup dark soy sauce for an hour or overnight.

2. Coat a Dutch oven or sauté pan with cooking oil and bring to a medium heat, brown the ribs in a several batches. Remove ribs and discard the excess oil.

3. Heat 2 tablespoons oil in the same pan, stir-fry ginger, green onion, star anise; add ketchup and cook a few minutes until the flavor are combined.

4. Place ribs back to the pan, add 1/2 cup white wine, remaining soy sauce, and crushed rock sugar. Add water to the level of the ribs, covered and bring it to boil.

5. Turn the heat to simmer and cook Wuxi ribs for one hour or until they are tender soft and almost falling off the bone. Check the rib periodically to make sure the liquid isn't dry-up.

6. Serve Wuxi Ribs with steamed rice or buns.

Yu Hsiang Pork

Ingredients: *(makes 8 servings)*

- ♥ 3/4 pound pork tenderloin or lean pork
- ♥ 1 cup dry wood ear, soaked and rinsed
- ♥ 2 carrots, shredded
- ♥ 2 celery stalks, shredded
- ♥ 2 teaspoons minced ginger
- ♥ 2 teaspoons chopped green onions
- ♥ 2 teaspoons minced garlic

魚香肉絲

Cooking Steps:

1. Cut pork into shreds and marinate with 1 tbsp soy sauce, 1 tbsp cornstarch and some cold water. Let it stand at least 15 minutes

2. Soak wood ear with hot tap water for half hour or leave it over night; rinse it thoroughly. Cut it into shreds.

3. Cut both carrot and celery into 2-inch long thin strips.

4. Prepare for seasoning sauce, in a small bowl, mix well 1 tbsp hot bean paste, 1 tbsp rice vinegar, 1 tbsp soy sauce, 1 tbsp white wine, 1 tsp brown sugar, pinch of salt, 1 tsp sesame oil, 1 tsp chopped scallion and 2 tsp cornstarch. Set aside.

5. Heat 2 tablespoons of oil, stir-fry pork tenderloin until meat is tender. Transfer pork to a plate.

6. Heat 1 tablespoon of oil, stir-fry the ginger, garlic and scallion for a couple of minutes. Add carrot, celery and wood ear, cook for a few more minutes. Bring cooked pork back and mix well.

7. Add seasoning sauce, heat it thoroughly.

8. Turn off the heat and sprinkle the chopped scallions. Taste and serve.

9. Tip: serve with tortilla wrap; make it like a spring roll. The uncooked flour Tortillas can be found in Costco and follow the instruction to cook it.

Fried Tofu Puff
with Glass Noodle Soup

Ingredients: *(makes 8 to 10 servings)*

- ♥ 1 pound fried tofu puff (prefer not the packaged)
- ♥ 1 package bean curd sheet (in frozen department of Asian market)
- ♥ 1 pound ground pork
- ♥ 8 cups chicken stock
- ♥ 2 (2-ounce) glass noodle
- ♥ 2 teaspoons rice wine
- ♥ 2 tablespoons chopped green onion
- ♥ 1 egg
- ♥ 1 tablespoon soy sauce
- ♥ 1/2 teaspoon baking soda
- ♥ Szechuan preserved vegetable, shredded
- ♥ 1 egg sheet, shredded

油豆腐粉絲湯

Cooking Steps:

1. Rinse tofu puff with hot tap water; squeeze it hard to get rid of its excess oil. Rinse again, drain and squeeze off water, dry with paper towel.

2. Soak bean curd sheets in hot tap water with baking soda. When the color changes and the texture turns soft, remove immediately and rinse off several times and drain. If the sheets are large, cut them into 6-inch squares, approximately.

3. For meat filling, season ground pork with green onion, egg, salt, rice wine and soy sauce, mix well.

4. Soak glass noodles with warm tap water and drain.

5. Stuffing 1/2 tbsp of meat filling into each tofu puff and lay them in a cooking container. Steam them in a steamer or a rice cooker for 20 minutes.

6. For bean curd sheets, (1) with stuffing, put 1/2 tbsp of meat filling in center of each sheet; roll it like to make a spring roll; (2) without stuffing, cut sheet in half, roll up and tie a knot. Place the meat rolls in a separate cooking container and steam for 20 minutes. All above steps can be done days before.

7. Before serving, boil chicken stock in a big pot, drop off number of tofu puffs and bean curd sheet wraps/knots into the pot and bring to boil. Cover with lid and let it simmer for 20 minutes. Before turn off heat, drop in glass noodles and cook for a few minutes until soft, taste for seasonings.

8. To serve, sprinkle green onion at bottom of a soup bowl, add soup and glass noodles. Float a few pieces of stuffed tofu puffs and bean curd rolls on top. Sprinkle more chopped green onion, shredded radish and egg sheet for garnish.

9. The unused tofu puffs and bean curd rolls can be refrigerated for later use.

Noodles in Soup
with Spicy Beef Stew

Ingredients: *(makes 6 to 8 servings)*

- ♥ 2 pounds beef shank
- ♥ 8 cloves large garlic, crushed
- ♥ 1 fresh ginger, sliced
- ♥ 1/2 teaspoon peppercorn
- ♥ 6 pieces dried red pepper
- ♥ 3 cloves star anise
- ♥ 2 teaspoons sugar
- ♥ 3 stalks scallions, chopped and divided
- ♥ 1/2 cup hot bean paste
- ♥ 1/4 cup regular bean paste
- ♥ 1/2 cup wine
- ♥ 8 ounces fresh noodles or spaghettis
- ♥ 1 can soup stock
- ♥ Salt and soy sauce
- ♥ 2 tablespoons diced pickled cabbage (cooked)

Cooking Steps:

1. Place beef shank, uncut, in a large heavy pot, add water and bring to boil; water should cover the entire beef. Turn heat to a medium high, add wine and green onion and continue to cook for 30 minutes.

2. Remove the beef and let it cool. Cut beef in 11/2-inch cubes, put them back to the pot.

3. Heat a tablespoon oil in a sauce pan, add sugar and stir; cook until it changes color. Add in garlic, ginger, green onion, star anise, peppercorn and red pepper and stir-fry for a couple of minutes until the aromatic smell is out; add hot bean paste, regular bean paste and wine. Cook a few minutes more then transfer it to beef stew pot. Continue to simmer, covered, until beef is tender (about 1.5 hours). Taste for seasoning.

4. Before serving, cook noodles by following the cooking direction on the package, cook until tender.

5. Meanwhile bring soup stock to boil. At the bottom of individual bowls, season with a little soy sauce or salt, sprinkle some scallion; pour half cup of soup broth over. You may use a large bowl for serving in family style; just add more soup broth.

6. Place cooked noodles in soup bowl; then add beef stews and the sauce on top. Garnish with scallions, green veggies and diced pickled cabbage. Serve immediately.

Stir-Fried Rice Cake
Shanghai Style

Ingredients: *(makes 8 to 10 servings)*

- ♥ 1 package rice cake (frozen)
- ♥ 8 ounces pork tenderloin, shredded
- ♥ 3 stalks green onion, shredded
- ♥ 1 king oyster mushroom, shredded
- ♥ 1 fresh bamboo shoot, shredded (if in season)
- ♥ 1 carrot, shredded (if bamboo shoot is not available)
- ♥ 3 dried mushrooms, soaked and shredded
- ♥ 2 jalapeños, seeded and shredded
- ♥ 2 shallots, shredded
- ♥ 1 tablespoon white wine
- ♥ 1 tablespoon soy sauce
- ♥ 3 tablespoons chicken stock or water
- ♥ Sesame oil

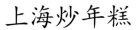 上海炒年糕

Cooking Steps:

1. Soak rice cake for 5 minutes. Drop into the boiling water for a minute or two until soft and tender. Rinse with cold water and drain, set aside.

2. Marinate pork tenderloin with 2 teaspoons soy sauce, pinch of salt, and wine for 10 minutes.

3. Heat oil in a sauce pan, sauté dry and fresh mushrooms and bamboo shoots (or carrots), add wine and stir well. Season with salt, transfer to a plate.

4. Heat oil in same sauce pan over a high heat. Sauté shallots and jalapeño for 30 seconds, add pork and stir for few minutes, then add white wine for flavor.

5. Bring all cooked vegetables back to sauce pan, stir them thoroughly until all flavors are combined. Taste for seasoning. Transfer half of it to the plate.

6. Add chicken stock or water with a teaspoon of soy sauce into the sauce pan; bring to boil. Place rice cake to sauce pan, toss and stir quickly so that each piece of rice cake will coat with meat sauce.

7. Add back the remaining pork and vegetables, and toss them well. Sprinkle with shredded green onion, drop 3 drops of sesame oil. Serve it immediately.

8. Tip: for a simple version, you only need one or two vegetables cooked with pork to make this dish. You may also add snow peas, green pepper, spinach or other greens to contrast the color for garnish.

Stir-Fried Rice Sticks with Shrimp

Ingredients: *(makes 8 to 10 servings)*

- ♥ 1 pound medium size shrimps, shelled and devein
- ♥ 8 ounces pork tenderloin or chicken breast
- ♥ 1 package dried rice stick (the product from Taiwan)
- ♥ 1 large carrot (or fresh bamboo), shredded
- ♥ 2 celery stalks, shredded
- ♥ 1 cup green, yellow or orange pepper (optional)
- ♥ 1 cup bean sprouts
- ♥ 3 fresh or dried mushrooms (optional)
- ♥ 1 tablespoon dried shrimp, soaked and drained
- ♥ 3 shallots, finely chopped
- ♥ 1 jalapeño, finely sliced
- ♥ 4 stalks scallions, half chopped and half thinly sliced
- ♥ 1 clove garlic, minced
- ♥ 1 cup chicken stock or water

蝦仁炒米粉

Cooking Steps:

1. Marinate shrimp with 1 egg white, salt, 1 tbsp white wine and pinch of cornstarch.

2. Shred pork tenderloin; marinate with 1 tsp soy sauce, 1 tbsp white wine and pinch of cornstarch.

3. Soak rice noodles in warm tap water for a few minutes until soft, drain, set aside.

4. Thinly slice the mushrooms, carrot, celery, pepper, jalapeño and green onions.

5. In a sauté pan, heat oil on high, stir-fry shrimps until the color changes; remove. Heat oil again, sauté 1/3 shallots for 30 seconds, stir-fry mushrooms, and all vegetables until tender. Season to taste, remove.

6. Heat oil, sauté 1/3 shallots, jalapeño, and garlic, add pork and stir for 3 minutes. Return cooked vegetables and toss until all flavors are combined.

7. In a large deep sauce pan, sauté chopped scallion, 1/3 shallots and dried shrimp for a few minutes until aromatic. Deglaze the pan with wine, add chicken stock and soy sauce, bring to boil. Drop soaked rice noodles, use wooden spoons or chopsticks to lift and toss so the sauce can be coated evenly. Turn the heat to low, cover and cook for two minutes or until the noodles are fully cooked.

8. Place half of cooked meat and vegetables to the noodles and toss more. Add chicken stock, water or oil, if needed, to prevent the rice noodles from sticking. Cover and cook more.

9. Return cooked shrimp to the noodles add sliced scallions and toss well, taste for seasonings. If rice noodles are hard, add more stock or water and cook over low heat for 2 more minutes.

10. Transfer to a plate, place the remaining cooked meat and vegetables on top; garnished with more chopped scallions. Serve immediately.

Sweet Rice
with Chinese Sausage

Ingredients: *(makes 12 servings)*

- ♥ 3 cups sweet rice
- ♥ 1 can of chicken broth
- ♥ 2 pieces of Chinese sausage, diced
- ♥ 4 ounces ham, diced
- ♥ 2 tablespoons dry shrimp or dry scallop
- ♥ 6 dried black mushrooms, soaked and diced
- ♥ 2 shallots, finely chopped
- ♥ 2 stalks green onions, finely chopped
- ♥ 3 tablespoons white wine
- ♥ 2 tablespoons water
- ♥ 1/2 teaspoon salt
- ♥ 1 tablespoon soy sauce
- ♥ 2 tablespoons cooking oil
- ♥ 5 pieces baby bok choy, cut in half for garnish

Cooking Steps:

1. Soak sweet rice with tap cold water for 2 hours; drain and transfer into a large microwave oven safe bowl.

2. In a small bowl, soak dry shrimp or dry scallop with cold water for an half hour, drain and chop into small pieces. Reserve the soaked water.

3. Pour one can of chicken broth into rice bowl and mix well.

4. Cook rice in **microwave oven** for 13 minutes with high power. Stir it at half way through and turn around (180°), if microwave oven does not turn automatically.

5. While sweet rice is cooking, sauté shallots and green onions in a sauté pan, at medium high heat, for 1 minute. Add chopped dry shrimp and stir for a minute or until aromatic; add in mushrooms, sausage and ham and continue to stir until the flavors of sausage, mushrooms and shrimp are combined.

6. Pour in white wine, soy sauce, soaked (shrimp) water and 2 tablespoons water, cook for another 3 to 5 minutes until sausage meat is cooked and juice is evaporated. Taste for seasonings.

7. Transfer sweet rice into sausage mixture and toss them well. Garnish with some greens along both sides of dish.

Wonton Soup

Ingredients: *(makes 4 to 6 servings)*

- ♥ 8 ounces ground pork
- ♥ 1 package medium size wonton wraps
- ♥ 1 egg white
- ♥ 2 stalks green onions, chopped
- ♥ 1 tablespoon soy sauce
- ♥ 1 tablespoon sesame oil
- ♥ 1 tablespoon white wine
- ♥ 2 bunches of spinach
- ♥ 1 (32-ounce) low sodium chicken broth
- ♥ 1 pickled Szechuan Radish Chinois, shredded
- ♥ 1 egg sheet for garnish

菜肉餛飩

Cooking Steps:

1. Cook spinach in boiling water about 30 seconds, plunge into cold/ice water; squeeze out the water and chop finely. Squeeze again for excess water.

2. In a large mixing bowl, mix pork and cooked spinach with egg white, wine, green onion, soy sauce and sesame oil to make the wonton filling.

3. Prepare for egg sheet, oil the pan in medium heat; whisky one large egg, pour egg in as you make a crepe pancakes. Cut egg sheet in half, and fold in half before julienned into long strips.

4. Place 1 teaspoon of filling in the center of wonton wrap, using your fingers, lightly wet the edges of the wonton wrap. Fold corner to corner to form a rectangular, pinch together the longer side corners to shape like a yuan-bau (元寶). Or bring 2 opposite corners of the wonton together to form a triangle shape. Finish all wontons and set aside.

5. Boil a pot of water, drop wontons into the boiling water and quickly stir to avoid wonton stick at the bottom of the pot. Cover with lid and cook; add a cup of water when the water boils again. Cook until all wontons float.

6. While wonton is cooking, boil chicken broth with two cups of water in another pot.

7. To serve, sprinkle green onion and pinch of salt at bottom of a soup bowl. Scoop two ladles of boiling chicken broth into the soup bowl, then place a dozen of wontons on top. Garnish with shredded pickled radish and egg sheet strips.

BBQ Pork Pastry
(Cha Shao Su)

Ingredients: (*makes 18 servings*)

- ♥ 8 ounces cooked BBQ pork, diced
- ♥ 2 tablespoons soy sauce
- ♥ 1 tablespoon sugar (on your own level)
- ♥ 1/2 teaspoon sesame oil (optional).
- ♥ 1 teaspoon flour
- ♥ 1 teaspoon cornstarch
- ♥ 1/2 cup water
- ♥ 1 egg, beat with 1 teaspoon of water
- ♥ 1 package puff pastry
- ♥ 1 tablespoon sesame seeds

Preheat oven at 400 degrees F

Cooking Steps:

1. For the filling, mix soy sauce, sugar, sesame oil, flour, cornstarch and water, cook until it begins to thicken; add BBQ pork and mix well. Let it cool.

2. Open the puff pastry box and spread one sheet out onto a floured board; put the unused pastry dough back in refrigerator immediately.

3. Flatten out the dough a little bit, cut pastry into nine equal squares.

4. Fill a spoonful of BBQ pork filling in the center of pastry dough, brush edges with egg wash; fold and close the edge to form a rectangular shape of Cha-Shao-Su.

5. Put Cha-Shao-Su on the baking sheet. Crimp the edge with fork and press down to seal. It makes a total of 18 Cha-Shao-Su for one package of puff pastry.

6. Brush egg wash on top of the pasties and spread with sesame seeds.

7. Make a couple of diagonal slits with a knife on top to let air out while baking.

8. Bake for 20 minutes or until pastries are puffed up and golden brown.

Chicken Spring Rolls
Shanghai Style

Ingredients: *(makes 18 servings)*

- 1 bag of spring roll skins
- 12 ounces chicken breast, shredded
- 8 ounces medium size shrimp, shredded
- 3 dry mushrooms, soaked and shredded
- 1 bamboo shoot, shredded
- 2 carrots, shredded
- 2 celery stalks, shredded
- 1/2 bag bean sprouts
- 2 scallions, shredded
- Salt and pepper
- 2 tablespoons soy sauce
- 2 teaspoons sesame oil
- 2 tablespoons hot chili sauce or sweet and sour sauce for dipping

上海春捲

Cooking Steps:

1. Marinate chicken with 1 tbsp white wine, 1 tsp of soy sauce, and 1 tsp of cornstarch. Marinate shrimp with 1 tbsp of white wine and 1 tsp of cornstarch.

2. Heat 1 tbsp oil in a sauce pan, stir-fry the chicken for a minute, drain and set aside.

3. Heat oil, stir-fry the shrimp for a minute, drain and set aside.

4. Heat oil, stir-fry mushrooms, bamboo shoots, carrots and celery; season with salt, soy sauce and little water and cook about 2 minutes, covered.

5. Place chicken and shrimp back to the pan, stir a moment; add the bean sprouts and green onions, cook in high heat for another minute.

6. Thicken it with cornstarch water, remove and let it cool before to wrap.

7. Place a spring roll wrapper on a flat surface, place two corners vertically so it looks like a diamond. Spoon 2 tbsp of the filling near the bottom corner of the wrapper and fold up to enclose the filling. Fold both sides in, roll up to form a tight cylinder. Brush the top seam of the wrapper with cornstarch water.

8. Pour about 1-inch of oil in a skillet. Deep-fry spring rolls for 2 to 3 minutes each side, turn and continue to cook each side until golden brown. Drain on paper towels before serving.

Chicken and Shrimp Rolls
Vietnamese Style

Ingredients: *(makes 10 servings)*

- ♥ 1 cooked chicken breast, shredded
- ♥ 8 ounces medium shrimp, cooked
- ♥ 1 (2-ounce) dry bean thread vermicelli
- ♥ 2 carrots, julienned
- ♥ 10 leaves from green leaf lettuce
- ♥ 1 cucumber, seeded and julienned
- ♥ 1/2 cup toast peanuts, crushed
- ♥ 1/2 cup fresh cilantro
- ♥ 1/4 cup fresh mint (optional)
- ♥ 10 rice paper wrappers

越南式春捲

Cooking Steps:

1. Soak dry vermicelli in boiling water slightly until soft; remove and rinse in cold water, <u>drain</u> well. Cut into 3-inch strands.

2. Cut each cooked shrimp in half, lengthwise.

3. For the filling, line up the ingredients in order, shrimp, lettuce, carrots, chicken, vermicelli, cucumber, peanut and cilantro (or mint), and place them in separate containers.

4. Fill a large bowl with warm water. Dip rice wrapper into the water for a few seconds to soften. Shake off excess water with a towel. Lay wrapper on a flat surface.

5. Quickly place 2 shrimp halves in a row across the center, cut side up, place a lettuce on top of the shrimp in the lower half of the rice paper. Lay a bunch of carrots in the center of lettuce, followed by chicken, vermicelli, cucumber, crushed peanuts, and cilantro, leaving about an inch on each side.

6. Fold the bottom half of the rice paper wrapper over the filling. Holding it tight, fold both sides in. Then, roll it up to close the top, like a burrito.

7. Repeat the process to make a total of 10 rolls.

8. Slice each roll in half diagonally and serve them with dipping sauce in room temperature.

9. For dipping sauce, in a mixing bowl, whisk together the ingredients: 2 tsp soy sauce, 1/2 tsp sesame oil, 2 tbsp lime juice, 1 tsp lime zest, 1 tbsp brown sugar, 2 tbsp rice vinegar, 1 tsp minced ginger, 2 tsp honey, 1 tsp hot sauce and 1 tbsp chopped scallions. Allow it to sit 15 minutes. Season to taste.

Chicken and Sausage
in Lotus Leaves

Ingredients: *(makes 8 to 10 servings)*

- ♥ 3 lotus leaves, cut each in quarters
- ♥ 2 cups sweet rice
- ♥ 4 dried shiitake mushrooms
- ♥ 2 Chinese sausages
- ♥ 1 ounce ham, chopped (optional)
- ♥ 1 teaspoon dry shrimp, soaked and chopped
- ♥ 2 shallots, finely chopped (divided)
- ♥ 2 scallions, finely chopped (divided)
- ♥ 2 tablespoons white wine or dry sherry (divided)
- ♥ 1 teaspoon dark soy sauce
- ♥ 1 teaspoon light soy sauce
- ♥ 1 boneless, skinless chicken breast
- ♥ 1 teaspoon salt
- ♥ 1/2 teaspoon brown sugar
- ♥ 1 can (14-ounce) of low sodium chicken broth

雞肉荷葉包

Cooking Steps:

1. Soak lotus leaves in hot water for minimum one hour; rinse thoroughly and pat dry. Cut off the edges and bad part; divide each into four pieces.

2. Soak dried mushrooms until soft. Cut sausages, mushrooms and ham into small pieces.

3. Cut chicken into small cubes. Marinate chicken with dark soy sauce, 1 tsp wine, and a pinch of cornstarch for 20 minutes.

4. Soak sweet rice for two hours, drain and place rice into a large bowl. Add *two thirds* of chicken broth and cook in microwave oven with high power for 10 minutes, stir the rice during the cooking. Let it cool.

5. Heat oil in medium heat, stir-fry 1/2 chopped scallions and shallots; add chicken, stir for 2 minutes. Add white wine and 1/4 tsp brown sugar, cook until chicken is 80 percent cooked through. Remove.

6. To prepare the sausage stuffing, follow the cooking steps 5 and 6 in Sweet Rice with Chinese Sausage.

7. All above steps can be done the day before.

8. Lay out a lotus leaf in front of you. Spread one thin layer of cooked rice in the center of lotus leaf, and then add chicken and the sausage stuffing on top of the rice; cover with another thin layer of sweet rice, like to make a sandwich. Wrap the lotus leaf to form a square parcel, place them in the steamer.

9. Repeat the process, it will yield about 10 lotus leaf wraps. Steam over high heat for 15 to 20 minutes. Serve immediately.

Chinese Green Onion Pancakes

Ingredients: (*makes 6 to 8 servings*)

- ♥ 3 cups all purpose flour
- ♥ 1 cup boiling water
- ♥ 1/3 cup of cold water
- ♥ 4 stalks green onions, chopped
- ♥ 3 teaspoons salt
- ♥ 3 tablespoons cooking oil

蔥油餅

Cooking Steps:

1. In a large bowl, mix flour with 1 cup of boiling water and stir until water is absorbed. Continue to add 1/3 cup cold water and mix thoroughly.

2. Knead the dough well, let stand and cover with a damp towel for 15 minutes.

3. In a small bowl, mix chopped green onions with salt and cooking oil, ready to use.

4. Remove the dough to floured board, knead again until smooth; divide dough into 6 pieces (or more).

5. Take one piece of dough, knead and roll the dough out to about 8 inch round, as making a pie crust. Place about two teaspoons of green onion mixture over the dough, spread it from center to edge.

6. Roll up the dough to make a cylinder roll then form into a round snail shape, tucking the final end into the center of the dough. Use your palm to press down then roll out until a quarter inch thick. Continue to finish all pancakes.

7. Heat 1 tsp oil (or use cooking spray) in flat pan, place one pancake in the center, cover and cook for 2 minutes in med to med high heat. Flip over and cook 2 more minutes or until both sides are golden and crisp.

8. Cut pancakes into small pieces and serve.

9. Tip: you can keep cooked pancakes in low temperature oven (275°F) until all pancakes are prepared.

Chinese Pot Stickers

Ingredients: (makes 4 dozens)

- ♥ 1 pound ground pork
- ♥ 1 pound raw shrimp, peeled, deveined, and chopped
- ♥ 2 bunches any green veggies, e.g. spinach
- ♥ 3 stalks scallions, finely chopped
- ♥ 1 cup minced fresh mushrooms
- ♥ 2 egg whites
- ♥ 2 teaspoons minced ginger
- ♥ 2 tablespoons white wine
- ♥ 3 tablespoons soy sauce
- ♥ 2 teaspoons sesame oil
- ♥ 1 teaspoon salt
- ♥ Homemade or ready-to-use pot sticker wrap

家常鍋貴

Cooking Steps:

1. For filling: (a) combine pork, mushrooms and shrimp in a large mixing bowl and mix with egg white, cooking wine, scallions, ginger, soy sauce, and salt thoroughly; (b) blanch spinach in boiling water about 30 seconds, squeeze dry and chop finely, squeeze dry again; (c) add spinach to the meat mixture. Drop sesame oil in and mix it again. Cover and refrigerate until ready to use.

2. For homemade dough, follow the Chinese Green Onion Pancakes recipe. One batch of dough will yield approximately 4 dozen medium pot stickers.

3. Flatten each pot sticker dough to form a round shape; make the centers slightly thicker than the edges.

4. Put 1 tbsp of filling in the center then fold over to make a half circle, pinch the edges towards to the center then stretch out a little longer.

5. In a hot sauté pan coated well with oil, place pot stickers flat side down and cook until the bottom is browned. Depending number of pot stickers, add half cup to one cup water and cover. Cook until the water has gone and then reduce heat to medium low. Cook dumplings for another 2 minutes.

6. Serve pot stickers immediately with dipping sauce.

7. For dipping sauce: in a small bowl, mix 1/4 cup light soy sauce with 2 tbsp red vinegar, 1 tsp chili paste, 1 minced garlic, 1 tsp minced green onions, 1tbsp water and 1 tbsp chopped cilantros. Let it stand for 10 minutes before use. Keep the dipping sauce fresh in a sealed container for several days, in refrigerator.

Chinese Style Calzone

Ingredients: *(makes 6 servings)*

- ♥ 1 pound yellow or white onion, thinly sliced
- ♥ 1 cup chopped celery
- ♥ 1/4 cup extra-virgin olive oil or cooking oil

Meat Filling:

- ♥ 1 pound ground meat (pork, beef, turkey or chicken)
- ♥ 2 bacons, chopped
- ♥ 1 shallot, finely chopped
- ♥ 1 garlic, greeted
- ♥ 2 jalapeños, chopped
- ♥ 1 teaspoon cornstarch, mixed with water
- ♥ 2 tablespoons white wine
- ♥ 2 tablespoons soy sauce
- ♥ 1/2 teaspoon salt
- ♥ 4 stalks green onions, finely chopped
- ♥ 1 teaspoon greeted ginger

Yeast Dough: follow the Meat and Vegetable Bun.

烤黃金肉餃

Cooking Steps: *Preheat oven to 400 degrees F*

1. Heat oil in two sauté pans with medium heat to cook onions and celeries separately. Cook onions until caramelized, cook celeries until soft; these are the basic ingredients for the dish. Remove and let cool.

2. Marinate ground meat with salt, white wine, soy sauce, green onion, ginger and the cornstarch water for 20 minutes. Heat oil, sauté bacon, jalapeño and shallot; add garlic and ground meat, cook until meat color changed. Season to taste, set aside.

3. Roll out yeast dough on a floured surface, divide it into 6 pieces, or more. Roll each into a round shape, about 7-inch diameter. Spread a spoonful onion, celery and meat fillings onto one side the dough; brush the outer edge with water and fold dough over to enclose the filling. Roll up the edges with your fingers to close tightly to form a calzone. Make a few cuts at top to allow air to escape during baking. Brush top with olive oil or cooking oil, sprinkle with sesame seeds if you desired. Spray the baking sheet with olive oil and transfer the calzone on it.

4. Bake 16 to 18 minutes until golden brown, rest 10 minutes. Cut and serve warm.

5. To make other fillings, try these ingredients in addition to the onion and celery mixtures.

♦ Veggie filling: bean thread vermicelli, scramble eggs, fresh mushrooms, etc.

♦ Seafood filling: red, green or yellow peppers, shrimp, salmon, or cod fillet, etc.

7. Tip: serve calzone with salad or soup. Store leftovers in refrigerator, reheat in toast oven for 5 minutes. They taste as good as fresh ones.

Chinese Turnip Pastry

Ingredients: *(makes 40 pastries)*

- 3 medium size turnips, finely shredded
- 4 ounces ham, finely diced
- 3 stalks green onions, finely minced
- 2 teaspoons salt
- 1/2 cup sesame seeds, white and black
- 1 egg yolk, mix with 2 drops dark soy sauce and 1/4 teaspoon honey for egg wash

Outer Layer (OL) Pastry:
- 3 cups flour
- 1/2 cup Crisco Shortening or vegetable oil
- 1 cup water
- 1 teaspoon sugar
- 1 teaspoon baking powder

Inner Layer (IL) Pastry:
- 2 cups flour
- 2/3 cup Crisco Shortening or vegetable oil

蘿蔔絲酥餅

Cooking Steps: *Preheat oven at 400 degrees F*

For the filling:

1. Shred turnips, sprinkle salt over and soak for 2 hours or overnight in refrigerator. Squeeze to dry, ready to use.
2. Heat 2 tbsp oil in a medium sauté pan; stir-fry ham and green onions for 2 minutes. Add turnips and stir for 2 more minutes until well mixed. Season to taste, transfer to a bowl and let it cool before use.

For the dough:

3. To make the OL dough: mix flour with shortening, water, sugar and baking powder in a mixing bowl, and knead into OL pastry dough. Cover; let it sit for 30 minutes.
4. To make the IL dough: mix flour with shortening in a separate bowl, and knead into the IL pastry dough. Cover; let it sit for 30 minutes.

For the Turnip Pastry:

5. Remove the OL dough onto a floured board and knead, divide it into 4 pieces. Do same process for IL dough. Take one piece of OL dough, flat it out; place a piece of IL dough in the center and wrap it up like a ball. Finish all 4 balls and ready to make.
6. For each ball, roll it out into an oval/rectangular shape (about 4"x 12"); then roll the longer side up into a thick cylinder. Sprinkle more flour on board, place cylinder in horizontal direction. Press down the cylinder with your palm, and roll out into one-eighth inch thick disc shape. Roll up the dough in vertical direction from one cylinder end to another to form a long thin jelly roll.
7. Divide the roll into 10 equal pieces, place the cut side up then press down to flat round. Roll out each piece into round shape, 3.5" in diameter. Place 1 tablespoonful filling in the center, close and seal with your thumb and index finger. Flatten into a 2" diameter pastry. Place pastry on the cooking sheet. Repeat steps 6 and 7 until all pastries are done. Brush top with egg wash then coat with sesame seeds.
8. Bake in oven for 10 minutes then turn to broil for 3 to 5 minutes or until golden brown. Serve warm.

Eight-Treasure Taro Pudding

Ingredients: *(makes 2 puddings)*

- ♥ 3 pounds taro root
- ♥ 2 dozens dried red dates
- ♥ 2 dozens dried lotus seeds
- ♥ 1 (18-ounce) can red bean paste
- ♥ 1/2 cup raisins
- ♥ 12 candied cherries
- ♥ 1 box mixed color candied fruits
- ♥ 1/2 cup brown sugar
- ♥ 2 tablespoon shortening or vegetable oil
- ♥ 1 teaspoon vanilla extract
- ♥ 1 teaspoon orange zest

Cooking Steps:

1. Prepare two medium size of molds or bowls. Lightly coat oil over the bottom and sides of each mold.

2. Soak red dates for 5 minutes, cook in a low heat for 10 minutes or until soft; cut in halves and remove seeds. Save the soaked water.

3. Rinse lotus seeds in cold tap water. Boil it on stove, turn heat to medium, continue to cook for 15 minutes or until soft and tender.

4. Soak raisins in water or desert wine, let it soft. Cut candied fruits in same sizes. These 3 steps can be done days ahead.

5. Arrange all decorated ingredients in a pretty design at bottom of each mold.

6. Clean and peel taro root, cut into thinly slices. Steam for 25 minutes or until tender and soft.

7. While taro is still warm, using potato masher mash taro with sugar and shortening until creamy and smooth. Discard the pieces that aren't soft. Divide mashed taro in two equal parts.

8. For each pudding, take two-third of taro to cover the bottom and sides, completely, up to the top of mold; leave the center empty. Fill center with red bean paste, up to 4/5 the way. Cover and close the gap with remaining mashed taro, flat it.

9. Steam taro pudding for an hour, check occasional if more water is needed. Meanwhile, mix sugar, corn-starch and the soaked (red dates) water to make the syrup. Bring to boil and simmer for 10 minutes.

10. To serve, turn mold out onto a serving plate. Pour the syrup over and serve hot.

Ground Beef Meat Pie

Ingredients: (makes 18 servings)

- ♥ 11/2 pounds ground beef
- ♥ 3 stalks green onions, finely chopped
- ♥ 2 egg whites
- ♥ 2 teaspoons minced ginger
- ♥ 2 tablespoons white wine
- ♥ 3 tablespoons soy sauce
- ♥ 2 teaspoons sesame oil
- ♥ 1 teaspoon salt

Dough: follow the Chinese Green Onion Pancakes.

Cooking Steps:

1. In a large mixing bowl, combine beef, egg white, cooking wine, green onions, ginger, soy sauce, sesame oil and salt. Stir them in <u>one</u> direction for 3 to 5 minutes or until they are well mixed.

2. Cover and refrigerate until ready to use.

3. Divide dough into 18 pieces. Knead and roll each dough out to about 6-inch round, as making a pie crust; make the centers slightly thicker than the edges.

4. Put 2 tbsp of filling in the center then close and seal with your thumb and index finger. Flatten into a 2-inch diameter meat pie. Place meat pie on the cooking sheet.

5. One batch of dough will yield approximately 18 medium size meat pies.

6. In a hot sauté pan coated well with oil, place beef pies flat side down and cook until the bottom is browned. Flip over and cook for a couple more minutes.

7. Add 3/4 cup water and cover. Cook until the water has gone then reduce heat to medium low. Cook beef pies for another 2 minutes.

8. Serve immediately.

Meat and Vegetable Bun

Ingredients: *(makes up to 2 dozen buns)*

- 1 pound ground pork (or chicken)
- 1 bunch spinach, or any vegetables
- 6 ounces mustard greens (酸菜), chopped
- 3 stalks green onions, finely chopped
- 1 cup minced fresh mushrooms (optional)
- 1 egg white
- 1 teaspoon minced ginger
- 2 tablespoons white wine
- 1 tablespoon soy sauce
- 2 teaspoons sesame oil
- 1 teaspoon salt

Dough:
- 1 teaspoon sugar
- 1 package Fleishmann's Rapid Rise yeast
- 3 cups all purpose flour
- 1 1/4 cup warm water
- 1 teaspoon baking powder

菜肉大包

Cooking Steps:

1. In a large bowl, whisk flour with sugar. Dissolve yeast in warm water. Add yeast mixture to flour, stir until water is absorbed. Knead the dough until smooth; cover it with damp towel, let rise until doubled in size, usually about two hours.

2. In a large mixing bowl, combine pork, mushrooms, egg white, cooking wine, green onions, ginger, mustard greens, soy sauce, and salt, mix well.

3. Blanch spinach in boiling water about 30 seconds then rinse in cold water, squeeze dry and chop finely. Add to the meat mixture, drop in sesame oil and mix well. Cover and refrigerate, ready to use.

4. Remove dough to floured board, add baking powder and knead until smooth. Cover and let rest for 30 minutes. Remove dough to board; slice into three pieces. Divide each into 6 to 8 small pieces; cover with damp towel.

5. Roll or press each into a round shape; make the centers slightly thicker than the edges. Place one to two spoonful filling in the center; gather the dough to close up. Let buns rest for 5 minutes before cooking, cook in several batches.

6. (a) to steam, arrange buns in a steamer, lined with a wet cloth. Bring water to boiling then steam for 10-12 minutes. (b) to pan fry, coat oil in a sauté pan, arrange buns to cover the entire pan, but leave a space in between; brown the bottom for a minute. Add one cup water and cover with lid, turn heat to medium high, cook until the water is evaporated, lower the heat and cook another minute.

7. Tip: choose your own favorite filling to substitute. Or, use red bean paste filling to make the sweet red bean buns.

Orange Glazed Beef Jerky

Ingredients: *(makes 1 1/2 lb)*

- ♥ 2 pounds beef flank steak
- ♥ 1/2 cup brown sugar
- ♥ 1/2 teaspoon salt
- ♥ 1 teaspoon five spice powder (optional)
- ♥ 2 pieces of star anise
- ♥ 6 pieces of red hot peppers (more if you like)
- ♥ 6 oranges, juiced
- ♥ 1 tablespoon orange zest
- ♥ 1/2 cup dark soy sauce

果汁牛肉乾

Cooking Steps:

1. In a large sauce pan, add water to cover the entire beef steak. Bring water to boil and cook for about 10 to15 minutes or until no red blood shown.

2. Remove beef steak out the pan and let it cool for 5 minutes.

3. Leave about one cup of beef broth in the pot, save the rest for other use.

4. Add orange zest and juice, five spice powder, dried red pepper, star anise, soy sauce and sugar in the beef stock; bring them to a boil. Cook a minute or two, until all flavors are well combined.

5. Cut or shred the beef steak into about 3-inch long strings; place them back to the stock.

6. Turn the heat to high, cook and stir constantly until all the liquid is absorbed by beef jerky, about 20 to 25 minutes.

7. Lay the beef jerky onto a baking sheet and let it cool in the room temperature. Or, dry it fast, you may bake in a low temperature oven (275°F) for 10 minutes.

8. Let it cool completely before keep in an airtight container. Beef jerky can be stored in refrigerator and served as a great snack in all occasions.

Pork and Mushroom Zongzi

Ingredients: *(makes 12 to 15 servings)*

- ♥ 30 large bamboo leaves
- ♥ 21/2 cups of sweet rice
- ♥ 11/2 pounds tender pork
- ♥ 12 dry black mushrooms, soak until soft, sliced
- ♥ 3 ounces dry shrimp, soak and clean.
- ♥ 3 tablespoons light soy sauce
- ♥ 3 tablespoons dark soy sauce
- ♥ 2 tablespoons cooking wine
- ♥ 1 teaspoon salt
- ♥ 1 package of string, for binding the zongzi

香菇肉粽子

Cooking Steps:

1. Cut pork in large pieces (1"x2"x3/4"). Marinate with salt, light and dark soy sauce, and cooking wine for minimum an hour or overnight for best.

2. Soak rice for two hours, drain, mix with salt and soy sauce for an hour, overnight is recommended.

3. Soak bamboo leaves in kitchen sink for overnight, wash and rinse thoroughly; cut off stem at top.

4. Prepare 15 strings, cut each in 55-inch long.

5. Line up 2 bamboo leaves side-by-side lengthwise; overlapping 2 halves such that one leaf vein touches the edge of the other leaf.

6. About 1/3 from the round end, fold and fan the two leaves apart a little to form a pocket (some parts of leaves will be overlapping).

7. Scoop about 2 tablespoons of rice into this pocket and spread along the base of this pocket for about 3 inches. Lay meat, mushrooms and dry shrimp over the rice. Cover the filling with another 2 to 3 tablespoons of rice.

8. Grasp the pocket like a triangle in your palm with the sharp point away from you. Fold the remaining bamboo leaf over the pocket as if it were the lid of the container; fold the side edges of this lid over the pocket to seal all corners.

9. Use string to tie the two ends tightly. The string should wraparound the bun 1/4 and 3/4 along its length.

10. Place zongzi in a big pot, cover over with enough water; boil them for 2 1/2 hours. Leave them in the pot for 10 minutes before draining. Serve it warm.

11. Keep zongzi in freezer up for weeks.

Shrimp Siu Mai Dumpling

Ingredients: *(makes 2 dozens Siu Mai dumplings)*

- ♥ 3/4 pound shrimp, shelled and deveined
- ♥ 1/4 pound ground pork
- ♥ 5 fresh mushrooms, finely chopped
- ♥ 2 stalks green onions, finely minced
- ♥ 1 teaspoon grated ginger
- ♥ 1 egg white
- ♥ 1 tablespoon low-sodium soy sauce
- ♥ 1 teaspoon Chinese rice wine or dry sherry
- ♥ 1/2 teaspoon cornstarch
- ♥ 1 teaspoon sesame oil
- ♥ 1 package round Siu Mai wrapper
- ♥ 1 large round parchment paper or cheesecloth
- ♥ 1 egg sheet, for garnish

Cooking Steps:

1. For egg sheet, follow the Wonton Soup recipe. Set aside.

2. Mince mushrooms, bamboo shoot and green onion, finely. Clean and shelled shrimp, cut them finely.

3. Prepare for the filling: in a large bowl, combine ground pork, shrimp, bamboo shoot and mushrooms with egg white, green onion, ginger, cornstarch and sherry. Stir in all seasonings and mix well.

4. Take one wrapper in hand; wet the edges with cold water. Put a teaspoon of filling in the center. Use your fingers, lift the edges of the wrapper up around the filling then squeeze the sides slightly, so the filling is partially exposed on top. Place the dumpling on the cooking sheet. Repeat with the remaining Siu Mai.

5. Place wet cheesecloth or parchment paper in the bottom of a steamer; lay dumplings on the cheesecloth, leave space in between so the dumplings will not touch each other.

6. Decorate Siu Mai with egg strings on top. Steam over boiling water for 10 to 12 minutes or until the filling is cooked through.

7. Serve immediately.

Simple Sweet Mochi

Ingredients: (makes 12 servings)

- ♥ 2 cups glutinous rice powder
- ♥ 1/4 cup cornstarch
- ♥ 1/4 cup sugar
- ♥ 1 cup cold water
- ♥ 1/3 teaspoon grated orange zest
- ♥ 1/2 teaspoon pure vanilla extract
- ♥ 1/4 cup coconut flakes or crushed peanuts
- ♥ 12 baking cups
- ♥ 1 tablespoon vegetable oil

For Fillings:
- ♥ 1/2 can red beans (paste), Or
- ♥ Combine these ingredients and mix well
    - ♦ 1/2 can lotus paste
    - ♦ 1/4 cup toasted ground almonds or peanuts
    - ♦ 1/4 cup toasted ground sesames

紅豆 Mochi

Cooking Steps:

1. For the filling, divide either red beans paste or lotus paste mixture into 12 pieces; roll each piece like a small ball. Refrigerate for cooling, you can do this hours or day ahead.

2. In a mixing bowl, mix together the rice flour, sugar, orange zest, vanilla extract and water, the rice mixture should be moving around, but not stiff.

3. There are several ways to cook the dough: (a) cook in micro wave oven for 7 to 8 minutes, or until it is done, stir at half way, (b) steam on stove or in rice cooker, for 15 to 20 minutes, or until the rice flour changes its color, (c) heat vegetable oil in a flat pan with medium high heat, pour rice mixture in, stir constantly and cook for 10 minutes or until rice flour cooked through (add water if needed). Let it cool down a bit.

4. Dust work surface with cornstarch. While rice flour mixture is still hot, begin dividing and rolling to balls. Flatten each rice ball and place 1 filling in the center. Pinch and close the mochi.

5. Coat mochi with shredded coconut flakes (or combine 1/2 cup ground peanuts with 1tbsp sugar mixture) and place the seam side down in the baking cups.

6. Serve and enjoy.

Sweet Red Beans Zongzi

Ingredients: *(makes 10 to 12 servings)*

- ♥ 30 large bamboo leaves
- ♥ 21/2 cups sweet rice
- ♥ 1 can (18-ounce) red beans (mashed)
- ♥ 1 package of string, for binding the zongzi

豆沙粽子

Cooking Steps:

1. Soak sweet rice for two hours, drain the water. Put in the refrigerator for use. Soak dry bamboo leaves in kitchen sink for overnight and wash it thoroughly; cut off stem at top. Prepare 12 strings, cut each in 55-inch long.

2. Divide red beans into 12 equal pieces; roll each piece like a ball. Refrigerate for cooling, you can do this hours or day ahead.

3. Line up 2 bamboo leaves side-by-side lengthwise; overlapping 2 halves such that one leaf vein touches the edge of the other leaf.

4. About 1/3 from the round end, fold and fan the two leaves apart a little to form a pocket (some parts of leaves will be overlapping).

5. Scoop about 2 tablespoons of rice into this pocket and spread along the base of this pocket for about 3 inches. Lay one red bean ball over the rice. Cover the filling with another 2 tablespoons of rice.

6. Grasp the pocket like a triangle in your palm with the sharp point away from you. Fold the remaining bamboo leaf over the pocket as if it were the lid of the container; fold the side edges of this lid over the pocket to seal all corners and edges.

7. Use string to tie the two ends tightly. The string should wrap around the bun 1/4 and 3/4 along its length. Place zongzi in a big pot, cover over with enough water.

8. Boil zongzi for 2 and half hours, leave it in the pot for 10 minutes before draining. Serve warm.

9. Keep zongzi in freezer up for weeks.

Instant Sesame Da-Bin

Ingredients: *(makes 8 servings)*

- ♥ 1 package fresh plain pizza dough (found in Trader Joe's)
- ♥ 1/4 cup sesame seeds
- ♥ 1 tablespoon olive oil or vegetable oil
- ♥ 1/4 cup chopped green onions
- ♥ Salt

Note: follow the recipe Meat and Vegetable Bun to make the home-made yeast dough.

芝麻大餅

Cooking Steps: *Preheat oven at 400 degrees F*

1. To rise the dough, follow the instruction from the package of fresh pizza dough.

2. Take the dough out from the package and put on a floured surface. Roll out it into 14-inch by 8- inch size.

3. Mix oil, salt and green onion in a small bowel, spread them evenly over the dough.

4. Fold/roll the dough three times, flat it. Brush oil on top and cut into 8 Da-Bin, coat each piece with sesame seeds.

5. Place Da-Bin on the oiled baking sheet, bake for 12 minutes; flip it over in halve way baking.

6. Remove from oven, allow to cool for 5 minutes.

7. Tip: to make one big round Da-Bin: (a) follow the steps of Chinese Green Onion Pancake recipe to make, coat sesame seeds on top, (b) follow the pan-fry cooking step in Meat and Vegetable Bun recipe to cook it on stove.

Sweet Rice Cake Squares

Ingredients: *(makes 2 dozen squares)*

- ♥ 1 pound package sweet rice flour
- ♥ 3 large eggs
- ♥ 1/2 cup cooking oil
- ♥ 2 1/2 cups whole milk
- ♥ 1/2 cup sugar
- ♥ 1 teaspoon lemon zest or orange zest
- ♥ 1 teaspoon vanilla
- ♥ 1 teaspoon baking powder
- ♥ 1 can (18-ounce) red beans paste
- ♥ 1 cup sliced almond
- ♥ 1/2 cup ground peanuts (optional)
- ♥ 1 tablespoon sugar (optional)

Preheat oven at 350 degrees F

方塊甜年糕

Cooking Steps:

1. Grease a 9-inch x13-inch baking pan with butter, from the bottom, sides, up to the edge.

2. Beat eggs and sugar well; add in remaining wet ingredients: oil, milk, vanilla, lemon zest and juice.

3. Stir in rice flour and baking powder, mix them well.

4. Pour the batter evenly into prepared grease pan.

5. Drop spoonful of red beans paste evenly over the batter.

6. Sprinkle sliced almond on top.

7. Bake the rice cake until the top is golden brown, about 45 to 50 minutes.

8. Let it cool for 10 minutes; cut into squares (a total of 24 squares).

9. Best serve when cakes are still in warm with tooth pick or fork.

10. Topping option: mix well the ground peanuts and sugar. Dip each rice cake square into mixture while cake is still warm.

Suzhou Crab-Yellow Pastry

Ingredients: *(makes 40 pastries)*

- ♥ 3 tablespoons cooked flour
- ♥ 3 tablespoons grounded almond
- ♥ 1/2 cup sugar
- ♥ 1 teaspoon vanilla extract
- ♥ 1 teaspoon salt
- ♥ 1/2 cup chopped ham or ground pork
- ♥ 21/2 cups chopped green onion
- ♥ 1/2 cup white or black sesame seeds
- ♥ 1 egg yolk, with 1/4 tsp honey, 2 drops soy sauce for egg wash

Outer Layer (OL) pastry dough:

- ♥ 2 cups flour
- ♥ 1/2 package yeast
- ♥ 11/2 tablespoons Crisco Shortening or vegetable oil
- ♥ 1/3 cup warm water and 1/3 cup boil water
- ♥ 1 teaspoon sugar

Inner Layer (IL) pastry dough:

- ♥ 11/2 cups flour
- ♥ 3/4 cup Crisco Shortening or vegetable oil

蘇州蟹殼黃

Cooking Steps: *Preheat oven at 400 degrees F*

For the filling: (make a choice)

1. Salty: in a small bowl, mix ground pork or ham with green onion, sprinkle salt over and mix well.
2. Sweet: in a small bowl, mix well cooked flour, ground almond, sugar and vanilla.

For the dough:

3. To make the OL dough: mix flour with hot water. Dissolve yeast in warm water, let cool for 1 minute. Stir in yeast water, shortening and sugar mix well and knead into OL pastry dough. Cover; let it sit for 30 minutes.
4. To make the IL dough: mix flour with shortening in a separate bowl, and knead into the IL pastry dough. Cover; let it sit for 30 minutes.

For the Crab-Yellow Pastry:

5. Remove the OL dough onto a floured board and knead, divide it into 4 large pieces. Do same for IL dough. Take one piece of OL dough, flat it out; place a piece of IL dough in the center and wrap it up like a ball. Finish all of 4 balls, ready to use.

6. For each ball, roll it out into an oval/rectangular shape (about 4"x 12"), then roll the longer side up into a thick cylinder. Sprinkle more flour on board, place cylinder in horizontal direction. Press down the cylinder with your palm, and roll out into one-eighth inch thick disc shape. Roll up the dough in vertical direction from one cylinder end to another to form a long thin jelly roll.

7. Divide it into 10 pieces, place the cut side up then press down to flat round. Roll out each piece into round shape, 3" in diameter. Place 1/2 tablespoonful filling in the center, close and seal with your thumb and index finger. Flatten into a 1.5" diameter pastry. Place pastry on the cooking sheet. Brush top with egg wash then coat with sesame seeds, using different color of sesame seeds for sweet or salty pastries. Bake for 10 to 12 minutes, then turn to broil for 3 minutes until pastries are golden brown. Serve warm.

Banana Pancakes

Ingredients: *(makes 8 to 10 pancakes)*

- ♥ 11/2 cups all-purpose flour
- ♥ 11/2 tablespoons sugar
- ♥ 1 teaspoon baking powder
- ♥ 1/2 teaspoon baking soda
- ♥ 1/4 teaspoon salt
- ♥ 2 eggs, separate yolks and whites
- ♥ 11/3 cups buttermilk
- ♥ 2 tablespoons melted butter or vegetable oil
- ♥ 1 tablespoon orange juice
- ♥ 1 tablespoon lemon zest
- ♥ 1/4 teaspoon vanilla extract
- ♥ Pinch cream of tartar
- ♥ 2 bananas, thinly sliced
- ♥ Vegetable oil or butter for cooking
- ♥ 1/2 cup maple or blueberry syrup
- ♥ 1/2 cup blueberry for garnish

Cooking Steps:

1. Combine all dry ingredients, flour, sugar, baking powder, baking soda and salt, in a large bowl and mix well.

2. In a separate bowl, combine egg yolks, oil, buttermilk, orange juice, lemon zest and vanilla extract.

3. Pour the liquid mixture into the dry ingredients; mix until flour is just incorporated.

4. In a medium bowl, beat egg whites with a hand electric mixer, add a pinch cream of tartar, beating until they hold soft stiff. Gently fold in egg whites to the batter. Let sit for 10 minutes.

5. Heat a nonstick pan over medium heat, add butter or oil to coat. Scoop a 1/4 cup batter into the pan place a few slices banana on top, cook for two minutes or until bubbles appear on the top surface and the bottom is golden brown.

6. Flip over and cook another minute until the bottom is lightly browned. Remove to a plate. Repeat with remaining batter. The unused batter can keep in refrigerator for up a day.

7. Garnish with more banana slices or fresh berries on top. Serve with maple syrup; or, dust with powder sugar.

Simple and Easy Delicious Crepes

Ingredients: *(makes 4 servings)*

- ♥ 1 cup flour
- ♥ 2 large eggs
- ♥ 3/4 cup milk
- ♥ 1/2 cup water
- ♥ 1 teaspoon orange zest
- ♥ 1/4 teaspoon vanilla extract
- ♥ 2 tablespoons melted butter and more for cooking
- ♥ Powder sugar for garnish

Cooking Steps:

1. In a large bowl, combine all of the ingredients and mix them until smooth. Let sit for 20 minutes. Stir again before using.

2. Heat a non-stick pan, add butter to coat. Pour 1/4 cup of batter into the center of the pan and swirl to spread evenly to cover the bottom of the skillet. Cook over medium heat for 1 to 2 minutes or until lightly browned and flip. Cook for another 30 seconds or until light brown, remove to the plate.

3. Fold the crepe in half and fold it in half again so that it has a triangular shape. Repeat this with all of the crepes. The unused batter can keep in refrigerator for a day or two.

4. Lay 2 to 3 crepes on a plate, sprinkle with powder sugar or serve with fruits or whipped cream on top.

Avocado and Mango Salad

Ingredients: (makes about 2 pounds)

- ♥ 4 big tomatoes
- ♥ 2 avocados
- ♥ 2 mangos
- ♥ 2 shallots, finely chopped
- ♥ 1 fresh lemon or lime, juiced
- ♥ 1 teaspoon lemon or lime zest
- ♥ 1 bunch cilantro, finely chopped
- ♥ 1 jalapeño, minced (optional)

Cooking Steps:

1. Peel mangos. Cut avocados, mangos and tomatoes into 1/2-inch cubes, squeeze lemon juice after avocado is cut. Put them in separate containers, ready to use.

2. Finely chop shallots and cilantro. Seed and mince the jalapeño. Ready to use.

3. In a large mixing bowl, mix together shallots, jalapeño, lemon zest, cilantro, mangos and tomatoes, except avocados.

4. Add avocado at last, season with a pinch salt.

5. Tip: this salad is good for all seasons. It also serves as a dip, with chips.

Chicken Salad

Ingredients: *(makes about 2 pounds)*

- ♥ 2 big chicken breast halves (cooked)
- ♥ 1 large apple or pear, peeled and diced
- ♥ 4 celery stalks, diced
- ♥ 2 small sweet pickles, finely chopped
- ♥ 1 jalapeño, minced
- ♥ 1 small shallot, minced
- ♥ 1 lemon, juiced
- ♥ 2 tablespoons finely chopped cilantro
- ♥ 2 tablespoons diced green onions
- ♥ 1 teaspoon hot sauce (optional)
- ♥ 1/2 cup toasted nuts, almonds or walnuts
- ♥ 1/2 cup cranberry
- ♥ 1/2 cup raisin
- ♥ Salt and pepper
- ♥ 3/4 cup mayonnaise, use more if you wish

Cooking Steps:

1. Follow Roast Tender Chicken Breast for cooked chicken breasts.

2. Cut or tear chicken breasts into large pieces, set aside. Chicken has to be cold before mixing with other ingredients.

3. In a big mixing bowl, put in chicken, apple, celery, sweet pickles, shallots, jalapeño, cranberries and raisins. Toss them well.

4. Mix them well with mayonnaise, lemon juice, green onion, salt, pepper, hot sauce and cilantro. Taste for seasoning.

5. Lay chicken salad on the bed of mixed green lettuce leaves, sprinkle toasted nuts on top before serving.

6. Chicken salad is a great dish for summer. You may serve it just for the salad dish, or use it to make the chicken salad sandwiches.

7. Chicken salad can keep in the refrigerator for a couple of days.

Mixed Berries Salad

Ingredients: *(makes 4 to 6 servings)*

- ♥ 1 cup sliced strawberries
- ♥ 1 cup blueberries ·
- ♥ 1 cup raspberries
- ♥ 1 bag fresh mixed baby greens
- ♥ 1/3 cup toasted sliced almonds
- ♥ 1 green onion, chopped

Dressing:

- ♥ 1/3 cup olive oil
- ♥ 2 tablespoons apple cider vinegar
- ♥ 1/4 teaspoon paprika
- ♥ 1 lemon, zest and juiced
- ♥ 1 tablespoon sesame seeds, toasted
- ♥ 1 tablespoon minced shallots
- ♥ 1 teaspoon honey

Cooking Steps:

1. In a medium bowl, whisk together honey, olive oil, vinegar, paprika, lemon zest and juice, sesame seeds and shallot. Cover and chill for 1/2 hour. You can make the dressing in a jar and just shake to combine.

2. In a large bowl, combine mixed greens, strawberries, blueberries, raspberries, green onions and almonds. Pour dressing over and toss. Season with a little salt and pepper. Refrigerate 10 minutes before serving.

Spinach Salad

Ingredients: (makes 4 to 6 servings)

- ♥ 2 bunches spinach
- ♥ 1 yellow or red pepper for color
- ♥ 1/4 teaspoon salt
- ♥ 1/4 teaspoon brown sugar
- ♥ 1 tablespoon soy sauce
- ♥ 1 teaspoon sesame oil
- ♥ 1 tablespoon crushed nuts

Cooking Steps:

1. Wash spinach thoroughly; drop it into boiling water for 30 seconds.

2. Plunge spinach into cold water immediately.

3. Squeeze out the water and chop; squeeze dry again. Put it in a mixing bowl with chopped red and yellow peppers.

4. For dressing, mix well soy sauce, sugar, salt and sesame oil.

5. Pour the dressing over the spinach salad and toss well, taste for seasoning.

6. Tip: spinach salad is an ideal side dish, serve with many dishes like Meat and Vegetable Bun, Instant Sesame Da-Bin, Chinese Style Calzone or Chinese Pot Stickers.

Supreme Tropical Salad

Ingredients: *(makes 4 servings)*

- ♥ 1 cup diced tomatoes
- ♥ 1 cup diced cucumbers
- ♥ 1 cup diced avocados
- ♥ 1 cup diced mangos
- ♥ 6 ounces baby shrimp
- ♥ 1 lemon

Dressing:

- ♥ 1/3 cup olive oil
- ♥ 2 tablespoons balsamic vinegar
- ♥ 1 teaspoon honey
- ♥ 1/2 lemon, juiced

Cooking Steps:

1. Prepare 4 ramekins, coat each with little bit oil. Ready to use.

2. In a small bowl, whisk together olive oil, vinegar, lemon juice and honey for dressing.

3. Cut tomato, cucumber and mango into 1/2-inch cubes, place them in separate containers. In each container, toss with 1 teaspoon salad dressing and ready to use.

4. Dice avocado into same size, squeeze lemon juice and mix well. Put in a container.

5. In each ramekin, place 2 tablespoons, each, of diced cucumbers, tomatoes, avocados and mangos, in order, to layer the salad. Refrigerate for 10 minutes. You may prepare this ahead the time and leave in refrigerator.

6. To serve, turn the salad mold out onto a plate. Scoop a tablespoon of baby shrimp on top and drizzle with more salad dressing. Garnish with more greens and serve.

Homemade Panini Sandwich

Ingredients: *(makes 4 servings)*

- ♥ 1 loaf of soft bread
- ♥ 2 tablespoons sweet butter
- ♥ 2 cloves garlic, finely chopped
- ♥ 2 yellow or red onions, sliced
- ♥ 8 thin slices sweet pickles
- ♥ 4 slices Swiss cheese
- ♥ 4 slices prosciutto or ham
- ♥ 8 slices home-made roast chicken or roast beef
- ♥ 1 jar roast peppers
- ♥ 2 avocados, thin sliced
- ♥ Fresh mixed green salad

Need a electric Panini grill

Cooking Steps:

1. In a sauce pan, sauté onions until caramelized. This can be done a day or hours ahead.

2. In a small bowl, mix well butter and chopped garlic.

3. Preheat Panini grill.

4. Using rubber spatula spread garlic butter mixture on one side of bread.

5. On unbuttered side of bread, layer Swiss, roast beef or roast chicken, prosciutto, cooked onion, roast pepper, sweet pickles and avocado or mixed greens. Sprinkle salt and pepper, if needed.

6. Cover sandwich with second piece of bread, buttered side up.

7. You can grill the sandwich immediately or you can wrap the entire sandwich tightly in plastic wrap and place in the refrigerator a day before cooking.

8. Place sandwich on pre-heated Panini grill and toast until bread is desired crispiness and cheese is melted, about 5 minutes.

9. Remove from grill and cut the sandwich in halves and serve; serve the sandwich with mixed green salad, using Simple Vinaigrette Dressing.

Lemon Shrimp Tea Sandwich

Ingredients: *(makes 18 sandwich)*

- ♥ 1 pound cooked baby shrimp
- ♥ 1 teaspoon lemon zest
- ♥ 1 tablespoon lemon juice
- ♥ 1/2 cup mayonnaise, divided
- ♥ 1/3 cup minced shallots
- ♥ 1/3 cup minced celery
- ♥ 1 teaspoon minced fresh tarragon leaves
- ♥ 1 package fresh chives, minced
- ♥ 1 big loaf of thin sliced white bread

Cooking Steps:

1. In a bowl, stir together the shrimp, salt, lemon zest, lemon juice, shallot, celery, tarragon with one-third cup mayonnaise.

2. Use a 2-inch round cookie cutter to cut out 2 rounds from each piece of bread. Finish to cut out all breads you need, cover with a sheet of plastic wrap.

3. Make sandwiches in 3 batches, do 6 sandwiches a time. Lay 12 slices of round bread cut-out on a clean work surface. Spread the shrimp salad on 6 slices round bread, and place remaining round slices atop of salad, pressing together gently.

4. Keep sandwiches covered with a sheet of plastic wrap to keep from drying out. Continue to finish all sandwiches.

5. Place minced chives on a small plate. Spread the remaining mayonnaise on the outer edges of sandwiches, coating well. Roll the coated edges in minced chives.

6. Tea sandwiches can be made 2 hours ahead, wrapped in plastic wrap, and kept chilled.

Papaya and Mango Salsa

Ingredients: *(makes 6 servings)*

- ♥ 1 ripe papaya
- ♥ 1 large ripe mango
- ♥ 1/2 medium red onion, finely chopped
- ♥ 3 tablespoons fresh lime juice
- ♥ 1 teaspoon lemon zest
- ♥ 1 small jalapeño, seeded and minced
- ♥ 2 tablespoons chopped fresh cilantro
- ♥ 1 red bell pepper, finely chopped
- ♥ 1 tablespoon extra virgin olive oil

Cooking Steps:

1. Peel, seed and dice papaya into small cubes.

2. Peel, seed and dice mango into same size of cubes

3. In a small bowl, toss papaya and mango cubes with red onion, lemon zest and lime juice.

4. Add diced jalapeño and cilantro, and drip some olive oil; taste for seasoning.

5. Cover and refrigerate for at least an hour before serving.

6. Tip: you may garnish Papaya and Mango Salsa on top of salmon filet dish, or use it as a dip for chips.

Semi-Homemade Rolls

Ingredients: (makes 18 rolls)

- ♥ 1 package of Bridgford frozen white ready dough
- ♥ 2 tablespoons unsalted butter

Cooking Steps:

1. Divide each loaf into 6 equal size pieces, roll each piece into a ball and placed them in a greased baking pan.
2. Brush dough with melted butter or spray with cooking spray.
3. Thaw dough in a warm place or covered in refrigerator overnight.
4. Let dough rise to double in size, about 3 to 6 hours.
5. Bake in preheated oven (375°F) for 20 to 25 minutes until golden brown.

Simple Vinaigrette Dressing

Ingredients: *(makes 4 servings)*

- 1 teaspoon of Dijon mustard
- 1 tablespoon balsamic vinegar
- 1/2 lemon, juiced
- 1 teaspoon lemon zest
- 1 teaspoon honey
- 1 garlic, chopped (optional)
- 1/3 cup olive oil
- Pinch of salt
- 1/2 teaspoon brown sugar

Cooking Steps:

1. In a bowl, beat balsamic vinegar with Dijon mustard, then add lemon zest, lemon juice, honey, garlic, salt and sugar until all ingredients dissolves.

2. Drip in olive oil and whisk constantly.

3. Taste and adjust the seasonings.

4. Refrigerate for 10 minutes before use. You may double the volume and keep in refrigerator for a few days, whisk before use.

Almond-Crusted Chicken

Ingredients: *(makes 4 servings)*

- ♥ 4 (6-ounce) chicken breast halves, boneless and skinless
- ♥ 2 eggs, lightly beaten
- ♥ 1 cup flour
- ♥ 2 tablespoons cooking oil
- ♥ 2 tablespoons salt
- ♥ 2 teaspoons water
- ♥ 1 teaspoon paprika (optional)
- ♥ 1 teaspoon garlic powder (optional)
- ♥ 1 cup raw sliced almonds
- ♥ Chopped fresh cilantro or chopped green onions for garnish (optional)

Preheat oven at 325 degrees F

Cooking Steps:

1. Rub entire chicken breast with salt. Refrigerate, covered for 40 minutes or over night.

2. Stir together flour, paprika and garlic powder in flat, shallow dish.

3. Beat eggs and water with fork in another shallow dish.

4. Put raw sliced almonds in 3rd dish.

5. Dip chicken into egg mixture then coat completely in seasoned flour.

6. Dip one side of chicken back into egg mixture again, coat with sliced almonds.

7. Heat oil in a sauté pan. Place chicken evenly with almond side up, cook 3 minutes with medium high heat. Then flip it over and cook again for 3 minutes until almond crust coating is golden brown.

8. Transfer chicken into foil-lined baking pan. Bake 20 minutes or until chicken is cooked through (juices run clear).

9. Cool it for 5 minutes; garnish with chopped cilantro or green onions. Serve almond-crusted chicken with mixed green salad or other vegetable side dishes.

Chicken Pasta Toss

Ingredients: *(makes 6 to 8 servings)*

- ♥ 2 chicken breasts, cooked
- ♥ 1 pound penne pasta
- ♥ 2 tablespoons extra virgin olive oil
- ♥ 2 cloves garlic, finely chopped
- ♥ 4 shallots, chopped in small pieces
- ♥ 1 big onion, diced
- ♥ 1/4 cup white wine or dry sherry
- ♥ 1 tablespoon lemon zest
- ♥ 1 lemon, juiced
- ♥ 1 cup chicken broth or water
- ♥ 1/2 cup fresh chopped parsley or cilantro
- ♥ Salt and pepper
- ♥ 2 scallions, finely chopped
- ♥ 1 red or yellow pepper, shredded

Cooking Steps:

1. You can either follow the recipe of Roast Tender Chicken Breast to roast chicken, or, buy whole Rotisserie chicken at store. When chicken is cool, tear chicken meat off the bone and break it into pieces.

2. Cook pasta, according the instruction on pasta package, for about 10 to 12 minutes until al dente; drain and put in a big pasta bowl. Stir in olive oil, parsley or cilantro, lemon zest and half lemon juice immediately.

3. Meanwhile, heat 1 tbsp cooking oil in a sauté pan with medium heat, cook onion for 5 to 10 minutes or until caramelized; transfer it to a plate.

4. Heat 1 tbsp cooking oil again, sauté garlic and shallots for about 2 minutes. Whisk in wine and half lemon juice; add a cup chicken broth, let it boil. Add cooked chicken, red pepper and cooked onion and cook for a minute or two. Adjust seasonings.

5. Transfer them to pasta bowl and toss it well. Finish it by dripping in more fresh lemon juice, extra virgin olive oil and garnish chopped cilantro or green onions on top.

Clam Chowder Soup

Ingredients: *(makes 8 to 10 servings)*

- ♥ 2 white onions, finely diced
- ♥ 4 celery stalks, finely diced
- ♥ 3 potatoes, finely diced
- ♥ 3 cans sea clam, chopped
- ♥ 2 tablespoons red wine vinegar
- ♥ 1/3 cup butter
- ♥ 3/4 cup flour
- ♥ 1 quart half and half cream
- ♥ Salt and pepper
- ♥ Paprika (optional)
- ♥ 1 bunch cilantro, fresh chopped (optional)
- ♥ Bacon bits (optional)

Cooking Steps:

1. In a large pot, add enough water to cover vegetables and cook over medium heat until barely tender, about 8 to 10 minutes.

2. Melt butter in a large sauce pan; add flour and blend, stirring constantly.

3. Add half and half cream in several batches, use wire whisk to whisk until thick and creamy, about 8 to 10 minutes.

4. Open cans of sea clam, separate juice and meat. Pour drained clam juice in sauce pan and stir for a few minutes.

5. Then, add vegetables in the pan, reserve the vegetable stock for later use, stir and mix well.

6. Add sea clams at last, pour a couple of red wine vinegar and heat through.

7. Season with salt and pepper to taste.

8. Ladle a big scoop to a soup bowl, sprinkle some paprika and add bacon bits if you desire. Garnish with cilantro.

9. Serve with fresh home baked rolls, see recipe Semi-Homemade Rolls.

Honey Glazed Salmon Fillet

Ingredients: (makes 6 servings)

- ♥ 2 tablespoons fresh lemon juice
- ♥ 2 tablespoons Dijon mustard
- ♥ 2 tablespoons honey
- ♥ 1 teaspoon lemon zest
- ♥ 11/2 pounds fresh salmon
- ♥ 2 teaspoons soy sauce
- ♥ 2 tablespoons chopped green onions
- ♥ 1 bag of fresh baby greens
- ♥ Cooking spray

Preheat oven to 400 degrees F

Cooking Steps:

1. Spray oil on the baking dish.

2. Slice salmon into 1-inch wide rectangle fillets

3. In a small bowl, mix soy sauce, lemon juice, Dijon mustard, honey, and lemon zest. Pour over salmon fillets in a large Ziploc bag and marinate for 45 minutes. You may use double bags to prevent leaking. Keep it in the refrigerator before baking.

4. Place salmon fillets in a baking dish, pour some marinade sauce over; turn salmon over to coat in more glaze. Sprinkle chopped green onion on top if you like.

5. Bake fish for 8 to10 minutes, then broil for 2 to 4 minutes or until fish is fork-tender.

6. Serve salmon fillets on the bed of baby greens and garnish with a handful of nuts.

Holiday Cornish Game Hens with Sweet Rice Stuffing

Ingredients: *(makes 4 to 6 servings)*

- ♥ 2 Cornish game hens
- ♥ 3 med-size yams (prefer purple color yam)
- ♥ 2 tablespoons butter
- ♥ Salt and pepper

Sweet Rice Stuffing:

- ♥ 2 cups sweet rice
- ♥ 2/3 can (14-ounce) chicken broth
- ♥ 2 Chinese sausages, diced
- ♥ 5 dried shiitake mushrooms, soaked and diced
- ♥ 2 shallots, finely chopped
- ♥ 1 green onion, finely chopped
- ♥ 1 tablespoon white wine

Follow the cooking method of Sweet Rice with Chinese Sausage recipe.

Preheat oven to 400 degrees F

Cooking Steps:

1. Season the game hens inside and out with salt. Place hens in refrigerator for an hour or overnight.

2. After sweet rice cooked, let it cool. This can be done a day ahead.

3. Cut yams in halves, lengthwise, and place cut side down at bottom of the roast pan.

4. Rinse hens inside and out with cold water and pat dry with paper towels.

5. Fill chicken cavity with sweet rice mixture. Tie the legs together with kitchen string and tuck the wing tips under the body; then place them, breast side up, on top of the yams in the roasting pan, alternating directions of hens so that they fit well in the pan.

6. Brush the outside of the hens with the butter, sprinkle salt and pepper and place in the preheated oven.

7. Roast hens for 25 minutes, brush with honey and soy mixture (1/2 tablespoon soy sauce, 1 teaspoon honey and few drops white wine); cover the pan with aluminum foil, continue to roast hens at 375°F for additional 20 to 30 minutes. Remove the foil and roast until the game hens are golden brown, and the juices run clear. And, a thermometer inserted into the center of the Cornish hen reads between 165 to 175.

8. Remove the pan from the oven and transfer hens to a serving plate. Cover loosely with aluminum foil for 10 minutes before serving.

9. Cut in halves or quarters, serve with sweet rice, cooked vegetables or green salad.

Pork Tenderloin with Orange Sauce

Ingredients: *(makes 8 servings)*

- ♥ 1 2-pound pork tenderloin
- ♥ 1 teaspoon olive oil
- ♥ 1 tablespoon unsalted butter
- ♥ 1 apple, sliced
- ♥ 2 tablespoons raisins, soaked
- ♥ 1 teaspoon brown sugar
- ♥ 1 orange, juiced

Marinade:
- ♥ 1/2 cup soy sauce
- ♥ 1/2 teaspoon salt
- ♥ 1 orange, juiced
- ♥ 1 tablespoon orange zest
- ♥ 1 lime, juiced
- ♥ 1 tablespoon Dijon mustard
- ♥ 1 teaspoon ground fresh ginger
- ♥ 1 clove garlic, crushed
- ♥ 1 tablespoon chopped scallions

Preheat oven to 350 degrees F

Cooking Steps:

1. Combine all marinade ingredients in a large bowl. Pour over the pork tenderloins in a large Ziploc bag. Marinate overnight.

2. Take meat out from the bag and use paper towels to dry the excess liquid, keep the marinade sauce for dressing.

3. Rub olive oil over the meat.

4. In a large skillet, heat oil with medium high. Sear evenly on all sides of pork tenderloins and cook 3 minutes each side, turning frequently.

5. Carefully transfer the tenderloins to the prepared baking sheet. Bake for 25 minutes. The inside meat temperature should be about 165°F.

6. Remove from the oven and let rest for 10 minutes, covered with foil before carving.

7. To serve, carve diagonally into slices in 1/2-inch thick. Spoon the dressing sauce onto each slice; garnish with Spinach Salad on side.

8. Tips: you may double this recipe for great leftovers, especially in making sandwiches. Please see next page for making pork tenderloin with stuffing.

Meat Dressing Sauce:

1. In a skillet, melt butter over medium heat. Add apple slices and raisins with orange juice and brown sugar, and stir for a couple of minutes.

2. Add the liquid of marinade sauce, cook in medium-low heat until the sauce is reduced to half.

Pork Tenderloin
with Orange Sauce (continue)

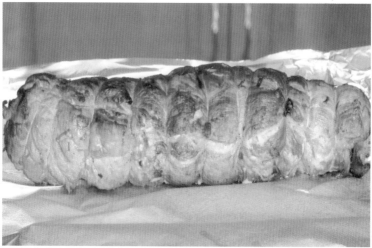

Ingredients: *(for Stuffing)*

- ♥ 2 tablespoons vegetable oil
- ♥ 8 shitake mushrooms, soaked and shredded
- ♥ 1 large bamboo shoot, shredded
- ♥ 4 pieces ham or prosciutto, thinly sliced
- ♥ 1 tablespoon soy sauce
- ♥ 1/4 teaspoon brown sugar
- ♥ 2 tablespoons white wine or dry sherry
- ♥ Some tooth picks
- ♥ One 4 feet long butcher's string to tie the meat

Preheat oven to 350 degrees F

Cooking Steps:

1. In a large skillet, heat with oil over medium-high heat. Cook mushrooms and bamboo shoots for about 2 minutes. Add soy sauce, wine and 1/4 cup water. Cover and cook another 5 to 10 minutes until juice is evaporated. Remove from heat let it cool. Set aside.

2. Cut the tenderloin lengthwise halfway through and open like a book. Line 4 pieces of ham in middle. Place the stuffing over, close the book with several tooth pick sticks to bring the pork tenderloins back to a roll. Tie the meat tightly with butcher's string, remove the tooth pick sticks.

3. Follow the same cooking steps on previous page. Remove the string before carving.

Roast Tender Chicken Breast

Ingredients: *(makes 4 servings)*

- ♥ 4 chicken breasts, with skin on and bone in
- ♥ 2 tablespoons salt
- ♥ 1 teaspoon pepper
- ♥ 4 tablespoons olive oil

Preheat oven to 325 degrees F

Cooking Steps:

1. Lay chicken breasts in a large roasting pan with the skin side up.

2. In a small bowl, mix together the salt, pepper, and olive oil; massage the mixture generously over the chicken breasts, both up and down.

3. Roast Chicken until internal temperature of the meat registers 160°F to 170°F on an instant-read thermometer; it takes about 35 to 40 minutes.

4. Remove chicken breasts out of oven and let it rest for 15 minutes before carving.

5. You can double the recipe to roast more chicken breasts and save them for making chicken sandwich, chicken pasta or chicken salad. Keep unused chicken breasts in refrigerator or freezer for later use.

6. Tips: if you use boneless and skinless chicken breasts , wrap chicken breasts with bacon strips and follow the same steps to cook.

Roast Prime Rib
with Baked Potato

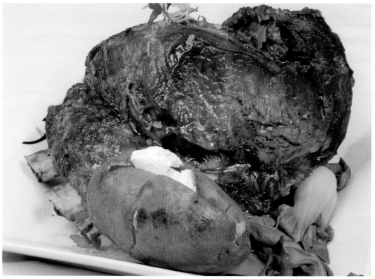

Ingredients: *(makes 8-10 servings)*

- ♥ 6 pounds bone-in prime rib roast
- ♥ 6 garlic cloves, sliced (optional)
- ♥ Salt and pepper
- ♥ 8 medium size potatoes
- ♥ Light sour crème or butter, for baked potato

Preheat oven to 350 degrees F

Cooking Steps:

1. Bring roast at room temperature. Season prime rib with salt and pepper.

2. Make small slits on top the prime rib and fill each slit with a slice of the garlic (optional).

3. Line a aluminum foil in a roasting pan, place prime rib, fat side up, in the center.

4. Transfer prime rib to oven and roast for 2 hours or until a thermometer inserted into the center of meat registers 140°F. It takes about 20 minutes per pound.

5. Let prime rib rest, covered with foil for 15 minutes, let the juice settle.

6. Remove prime rib to a carving board, reserve the juice for the gravy. Remove the fat oil on top before carving. Slice meat with an electric slicing knife and serve immediately.

Baked Potatoes:

1. Scrub potatoes and pat dry.

2. Poke holes in potatoes and wrap each in foil.

3. Place potatoes either on a separate layer of rack, or, outside the prime rib on roasting pan.

4. Bake for an hour and half or until the sides are soft when pressed.

5. Transfer to a plate.

6. Serve potato with butter or sour crème.

Roast Turkey

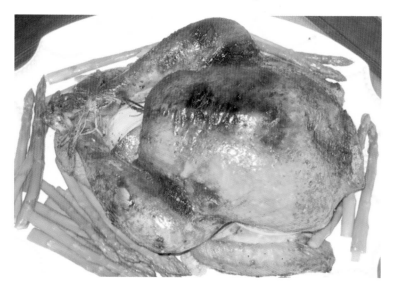

Ingredients: (makes 12 servings)

- ♥ 1 12-pound turkey
- ♥ 2 tablespoons unsalted butter
- ♥ 2 tablespoons fresh chopped scallions
- ♥ 1 teaspoon lemon zest
- ♥ 1 teaspoon chopped fresh cilantro (optional)
- ♥ 2 tablespoons olive oil or canola oil
- ♥ 1 tablespoon soy sauce
- ♥ 1 tablespoon honey
- ♥ 2 large sweet potatoes, or yams or carrots
- ♥ Salt and pepper

Preheat oven to 400 degrees F

Cooking Steps:

1. Take giblets out of the turkey and wash turkey inside and out. Remove any excess fat and use paper towel to dry. Rub salt all over the body including the inside of turkey cavity. Refrigerate it overnight. Rinse and dry it, ready to use.

2. In a small bowl, combine oil, soy sauce, honey, lemon zest and juice, cilantro and green onions together. Rub this mixture inside the cavity and under the turkey skin, especially in the areas of breast and thigh.

3. Tie the legs together with string and tuck the wing tips under the body. Soft the butter, rub it to outside the body. Sprinkle more salt over

4. Cut sweet potatoes or carrots in half, lengthwise; place them, cut side down, in the bottom of the roast pan. Place the turkey on top so that the turkey does not rest directly on the bottom of the pan.

5. Roast turkey at 400°F for 30 minutes, then lower the temperature to 350°F; cover with the aluminum foil and continue to roast 2 to 2 1/2 hours. Remove the foil, roast until the juices run clear when you cut between the leg and thigh. The inside meat temperature should be about 165°F to 175°F . Brush with oil and soy sauce mixture from time to time while roasting.

6. Remove turkey to a cutting board and cover with foil; let it rest for 20 minutes. Reserve the juice for gravy.

7. Tip: you can make turkey with sweet rice stuffing, the roasting time then will increase by an hour or so. To make the sweet rice stuffing, follow the recipe Sweet Rice with Chinese Sausage.

Easy Pan-Fried Salmon Fillet

Ingredients: *(makes 8 servings)*

- 2 pounds fresh salmon fillet
- 1 teaspoon salt
- 1 cup of flour
- 2 tablespoons cooking oil
- 2 stalks green onions, finely chopped
- 1 shallot, finely chopped
- 2 cloves garlic, minced
- 1/2 cup of white wine

Cooking Steps:

1. Cut salmon into 4-ounce rectangle fillets.

2. Season each fish fillet with salt and pepper.

3. Coat each salmon fillet lightly with flour, set aside.

4. Heat 2 tablespoons of cooking oil in a large skillet over medium-high heat. Place all salmon fillets in hot skillet and cook 2 minutes per side.

5. Add garlic, shallots and green onions in the middle of the skillet, stir a few seconds.

6. Pour white wine in and let cook another minute or until fork-tender. Sprinkle more green onion.

7. Serve with Papaya and Mango Salsa on top.

Seafood Cakes

Ingredients: (makes 10 to 12 servings)

- ♥ 3/4 pound fresh salmon or cod fillet, finely chopped
- ♥ 6 ounces shrimp, finely chopped
- ♥ 2 eggs
- ♥ 1 each, red, orange and yellow peppers, diced
- ♥ 1 tablespoon grated lemon zest
- ♥ 1 teaspoon lemon juice
- ♥ 2 cups bread crumbs, divided
- ♥ 1/2 cup almond meal (or use grounded almonds)
- ♥ 1 tablespoon white wine
- ♥ 2 teaspoons mayonnaise
- ♥ 2 teaspoons chopped ginger
- ♥ 2 teaspoons chopped green onions
- ♥ 2 teaspoons soy sauce
- ♥ 2 tablespoons freshly chopped cilantro

Cooking Steps:

1. In a large bowl, combine all the ingredients, fish, shrimp, eggs, peppers, lemon zest and juice, almond meal, mayonnaise, soy sauce, ginger, green onion, cilantro and 1/2 cup bread crumbs.

2. Put remaining bread crumbs in a flat, shallow dish.

3. Divide the mixture into 10 to 12 patties and form into cakes approximately 1-inch thick.

4. Coat each cake with bread crumbs and transfer to a baking sheet lined with waxed paper. The seafood cakes can be refrigerated overnight before use.

5. Place a medium size skillet over medium heat. Heat 2 tablespoons of oil, arrange cakes gently in skillet. Pan-fry first side for two minutes then carefully flipper over and pan-fry the other side 2 minutes or until golden brown.

6. Serve immediately with dipping sauce drizzled on top.

7. In the crab season, use fresh crab meat to make crab cakes, with same cooking steps and dipping sauce.

Dipping Sauce:

- ♥ 2 tablespoons hot sweet mustard or Dijon mustard
- ♥ 1/4 cup mayonnaise
- ♥ 1 teaspoon lemon zest
- ♥ 1 teaspoon fresh lemon juice
- ♥ 1 teaspoon finely chopped green onions
- ♥ 1/2 teaspoon grated ginger
- ♥ Dash salt, dash sugar

In a small bowl, mix all ingredients together. Refrigerate for 30 minutes before serve.

Simple Delicious Roast Beef

Ingredients: *(makes 8 servings)*

- ♥ 3 pounds cross rib roast beef or pot roast beef
- ♥ 2 tablespoons salt
- ♥ 1 teaspoon pepper
- ♥ Olive oil

Preheat oven to 325 degrees F

Cooking Steps:

1. Lay roast beef in a large roasting pan with the fat side up.

2. In a small bowl, mix salt, pepper, and olive oil together; pour over on top of roast beef and massage generously over the entire body.

3. Place roasting pan in the oven and roast the beef until the internal temperature of the meat registers 140°F (for beef rare) on an instant-read thermometer; it would take about 2 hours.

4. Remove roast beef to a carving board and let it rest for 20 minutes before carving; reserve the juice for gravy.

5. Homemade Roast beef is great for sandwiches. Freeze unused portion for later use.

Warm Delicious Chicken Pot Pie

Ingredients: *(makes 6 to 8 servings)*

- 2 chicken breasts, cooked
- 1 cup frozen peas
- 1 cup frozen soy beans
- 2 carrots, diced
- 1 onion, diced
- 3 celery stalks, diced
- 1 1/2 cups low sodium chicken broth
- 1/2 cup milk
- 3 tablespoons flour
- 1/2 teaspoon twenty-one seasoning (optional)
- 1/2 teaspoon salt
- 1 egg, for egg wash
- 1 package puff pastry

Preheat oven to 400 degrees F

Cooking Steps:

1. In a sauté pan, sauté the onions with medium heat for 5 minutes.

2. Add carrots, soybeans and celery, cook until vegetables are tender.

3. Add chicken broth, cook until boiling.

4. Meanwhile in microwave oven, heat the milk on high for about 40 seconds, add flour and whisk constantly to avoid formation of lumps.

5. Pour milk mixture into the sauce pan and cook in low heat until thickened.

6. Cut chicken in cubes. Add chicken and frozen peas in the soup, mix well; season with salt and pepper.

7. Divide the filling evenly into 6 to 8 ovenproof cups.

8. Cut each puff pastry dough into quarters. Brush the edges with egg wash. Place pastry dough on top of each cup, egg wash side down. Let dough hang over, then, press it to all sides. Brush egg wash on top pastry; make two cuts for air out while baking.

9. Place pot pies on a baking sheet and bake for 20 to 25 minutes, or until the top is golden brown and the soup is hot and bubbly.

10. Serve warm.

Cream of Carrot Soup

Ingredients: (makes 6 to 8 servings)

- 5 to 6 carrots, peeled and diced
- 2 onions, peeled and diced
- 4 celery stalks, diced
- 2 sweet potatoes, peeled and diced
- 2 tablespoons grated fresh ginger
- 2 garlic cloves, finely chopped
- 2 cans low sodium and low fat chicken stock
- 1 orange, juiced
- 1 teaspoon orange zest
- 1/2 cup half and half cream
- Salt and white pepper
- Sour cream for garnish
- Fresh chive or scallion, finely chopped for garnish

Cooking Steps:

1. In a large sauce pan (prefer cast iron cookware), over medium high heat, sauté onions and celery, add garlic in half way, cook until onions are soft.

2. Add carrots, sweet potatoes and ginger into the sauce pan; cover and bring to a boil. Reduce heat and simmer for 10 to 15 minutes until carrots are tender.

3. Add chicken stock, orange juice and zest, bring to a boil. Reduce heat to medium-low, cover and continue cook for 5 munities, stirring occasionally, until all flavors are combined.

4. Puree the soup, using a hand blender, until smooth. Soup should be thick. If you use the standard blender, do it in several batches. Also for your safety, let the soup cool to room temperature before put into the blender.

5. Return the soup to sauce pan. Stir in half and half cream, cook the soup until it is creamy and smooth. Add seasoning.

6. To serve, ladle into bowls; garnish with a dollop of sour cream and sprinkle with some fresh chives or scallion. Serve immediately.

7. Tip: this is an ideal soup served all seasons. Replace carrots for other vegetables like summer squash, zucchini or other vegetables during its harvest season.

French Onion Soup

Ingredients: *(makes 6 servings)*

- ♥ 3 to 4 large yellow onions, thinly sliced
- ♥ 3 tablespoons unsalted butter or cooking oil
- ♥ Fresh bay leaf, parsley and thyme, tied together
- ♥ 1 cup white wine or medium-dry sherry
- ♥ 1 teaspoon brandy or Cognac (optional)
- ♥ 4 cups beef stock
- ♥ 6 cups chicken stock
- ♥ 12 slices toasted French bread
- ♥ 6 to 10 slices Gruyere cheese or Swiss cheese
- ♥ Salt and pepper

Cooking Steps:

1. In a large sauté pan, sauté onions with butter or cooking oil. Cook on high heat for 5 minutes, stirring often, then turn the heat to medium; continue to cook until the onions are very soft and caramelized. It takes about 30 to 40 minutes.

2. Meanwhile, in a large pot, heat beef and chicken stocks with fresh herbs, bring them to boil then simmer.

3. When onions are ready, turn the heat to high; pour the Cognac and sherry wine, let the wine evaporated, about 3 minutes. Add stocks, bring to a boil, then simmer uncovered for 20 to 30 minutes. Remove herbs, taste for seasoning.

4. When ready to eat, preheat the oven to broiler. Toast the baguette slices for seconds.

5. On a baking sheet, place 6 small ovenproof soup bowls or crocks. Ladle the onion soup into each bowl, up to 3/4 the bowl, float toasted baguette slice on top, toast side down, and top with cheese.

6. Preheat oven, place soup bowls into oven under a broil until cheese melts and golden brown, which only takes about 2 to 3 minutes.

7. Carefully transfer the soup to each serving plate. Serve immediately.

Orange Glazed Yams

Ingredients: *(makes 6 to 8 servings)*

- ♥ 5 large yams or sweet potatoes
- ♥ 1/2 cup brown sugar
- ♥ 2 cups orange juice
- ♥ 1 tablespoon orange zest and some orange skins
- ♥ 2 tablespoons unsalted butter
- ♥ 12 to 15 large size marshmallows (optional)

Preheat oven at 325 degrees F

Cooking Steps:

1. Wash and rinse yams with tap water, leave the skin on. Place yams in a large pot, covered with water. Bring it to boil, then turn the heat to medium; cook until they are tender but not fall apart, about 20 minutes.

2. Remove yams to a plate and let it cool ; reserve a cup and half cooked yam water.

3. Peel off skins and arrange them into a deep baking dish. You may slice yams into large pieces, if yams are big, place cut-side up in the baking pan.

4. In a small pot, mix together the butter, sugar, orange juice and zest, and yam water. Cook until the liquid is reduced to two thirds.

5. Pour liquid over the yams, sprinkle marshmallows on top.

6. Place in a preheated oven and bake for 25 minutes until all marshmallows are melted and juice is reduced to a third or a fourth.

7. Serve immediately.

Pita Bread Served with Cooked Pork Tenderloins

Ingredients: *(makes 6 to 8 servings)*

- ♥ 1 pound cooked pork tenderloins
- ♥ 2 onions, sliced
- ♥ 2 teaspoons mashed garlic
- ♥ 1/2 cup white wine
- ♥ 1 tablespoon soy sauce
- ♥ 1 tablespoon cooking oil
- ♥ 8 ounces mixed green salad
- ♥ 1/4 purple cabbage, shredded
- ♥ 1 bag wheat pita bread

Cooking Steps:

1. This dish uses the leftovers of cooked pork tenderloins from the recipe of Pork Tenderloins with Orange Sauce. Slice the pork into thin pieces.

2. Sauté onion with 1 tablespoon of cooking oil, cook until caramelized, about 5 minutes. Add garlic and shallots in the middle of pan and continue sauté for about 2 minutes; whisk in 1/2 cup white wine.

3. Add pork in sauce pan and toss with onion. Season with salt.

4. Heat and soft pita bread in rice cooker or a steamer. Cut pita bread in half and open it like a pocket.

5. Mix green salad with Vinaigrette Dressing.

6. Mix shredded cabbage with a pinch of salt and olive oil.

7. To serve, place shredded cabbage at the bottom, green salad in the middle and the meat on top for the three layers pocket. Garnish with cilantro or other greens. Serve warm.

8. Tip: you may substitute pork with any cooked meat, like roast beef, roast chicken or salmon fillets.

Shrimp Strudel

Ingredients: *(makes 18 2-inch strudels)*

- ♥ 2 onions chopped
- ♥ 3 scallions, chopped
- ♥ 2 garlic cloves, minced
- ♥ 1 pound white shrimp, peeled and deveined
- ♥ 2 teaspoons fresh cilantro, chopped
- ♥ 1 lemon, juiced and zest
- ♥ 2 teaspoons canola oil
- ♥ 1 tablespoon unsalted butter or PAM oil spray
- ♥ 1 dozen Fillo dough sheets
- ♥ 1/4 cup plain dry breadcrumbs or almond flour
- ♥ Raw sliced almonds (optional)

Preheat oven to 400 degrees F

Cooking Steps:

1. Heat 2 tablespoons oil in a sauté pan, add the garlic and onion, cook over medium heat until the onions are soft, approximately 5 minutes, let it cool.

2. In a bowl, mix shrimp with cilantro, lemon zest and juice, and salt. Add onion mixture and mix well.

3. Unfold the Fillo dough sheets. Brush first sheet with melted butter (or spray vegetable oil) and sprinkle with bread crumbs or almond flour. Laying a second Fillo dough sheet over the first sheet, spray it with oil and sprinkle with bread crumbs or almond flour until 4 sheets have been used.

4. Spoon the shrimp mixture along the edge of the Fillo dough. Roll it up like a cylinder. Brush the top with butter or egg wash; sprinkle chopped scallions or sliced almonds on top, set aside. Repeat to finish 3 shrimp strudels.

5. Line a parchment paper on the baking sheet, transfer strudels onto it; bake them for 12 to 15 minutes, or until the top is lightly brown. Cut each strudel into 11/2-inch size and serve warm.

6. Tip: you can substitute shrimp with salmon, crab or veggies.

Sweet Potato Soufflés

Ingredients: (makes 6 servings)

- ♥ 3 medium sweet potatoes
- ♥ 3 tablespoons brown sugar
- ♥ 2 egg yolks, beaten
- ♥ 4 egg whites
- ♥ 1/2 teaspoon salt
- ♥ 2 tablespoons butter, divided
- ♥ 1/2 cup evaporated milk
- ♥ 1/2 teaspoon vanilla
- ♥ 1/4 teaspoon cream of tartar
- ♥ Some granulated sugar
- ♥ 1 tablespoon orange zest

Preheat oven to 375 degrees F

Cooking Steps:

1. Prepare 6 6-oz ramekins. Brush each with soft butter, then sprinkle with granulated sugar. Place ramekins in the refrigerator (this can be done hours ahead).

2. In a large pot, cook sweet potatoes over high heat until boiling; continue cook in medium heat until soft and tender, about 25 minutes. Let it cool for 5 minutes before peeling, then transfer it to a large mixing bowl and mash it.

3. In a small sauce pan, melt butter; add sugar and milk; stir about 2 to 3 minutes until the flavors are combined. Turn off the heat, add all remaining ingredients, egg yolks, salt, orange zest and vanilla. Combine them with sweet potatoes, mix until well incorporated. Set aside.

4. In a medium bowl, beat egg whites with a hand electric mixer, gradually add sugar (1 tsp) and cream of tartar, beating until they hold a soft stiff.

5. Place a third of the egg whites into the sweet potatoes mixture and gently fold in, then do the remaining whites in several batches.

6. Gently spoon mixture into prepared soufflé ramekins to 85 percent of the way full; make sure there is no air in between and smooth out at the top. Place them in a baking sheet.

7. Transfer to the oven and reduce the temperature to 350°F. Bake until they are golden and puffed over the edge, about 30 to 35 minutes.

8. Serve immediately.

Almond Biscotti Cookies

Ingredients: (makes 3 dozens)

- ♥ 1/3 cup white sugar
- ♥ 1/2 cup brown sugar
- ♥ 2 eggs
- ♥ 3 tablespoons soft unsalted butter
- ♥ 2 tablespoons pure vanilla
- ♥ 2 tablespoons orange zest
- ♥ 2 tablespoons fresh orange juice
- ♥ 1 teaspoon baking power
- ♥ 1 teaspoon cocoa powder (optional)
- ♥ 1/8 teaspoon cinnamon (optional)
- ♥ 2 cups all purpose flour
- ♥ 3 cups whole almonds
- ♥ 1 egg, for egg wash
- ♥ More flour for working surface.

Preheat oven to 350 degrees F

Cooking Steps:

1. Put eggs, brown sugar, white sugar, and butter in a large mixing bowl.

2. With mixer on low speed, mix in orange zest, orange juice and vanilla. (OR mix with a wooden spoon).

3. Sift dry ingredients: flour, baking powder, and cinnamon and cocoa powder; combine all dry ingredients with egg mixture until dough holds together.

4. Stir in almonds, mix well but not over mix.

5. Put dough on a floured surface. Divide in half. Roll each piece into a log.

6. Line a parchment paper on a baking sheet, transfer logs onto it.

7. Sprinkle little more flour on logs and flatten each log with hand. Lightly brush with egg wash over top.

8. Bake for 30 to 35 minutes until firm to touch. Let it cool for 10 minutes.

9. Cut dough diagonally into biscotti, it makes approximately 36 (3 /4 " by 4 1/2") biscotti cookies. Return biscotti to baking sheet with the slices cut side up. Reduce oven temperature to 300°F, bake until sufficiently dry, about 20 to 25 minutes.

10. Remove from oven and let it cool completely before serving or storing in a jar.

11. Biscotti cookies can be stored in the room temperature for a month.

Apple and Pear Turnovers

Ingredients: *(makes 8 servings)*

- ♥ 1 package of puff pastry .
- ♥ 2 pears and 2 apples, peeled, cored, and sliced .
- ♥ 1 egg, for egg wash.
- ♥ 1/2 cup raisins
- ♥ 1/2 cup sliced almonds.
- ♥ Confectioners' sugar for serving

Almond Paste:

- ♥ 2 tablespoons unsalted butter, softened
- ♥ 2 tablespoons sugar
- ♥ 1 egg yolk
- ♥ 1/4 teaspoon almond extract
- ♥ 1 cup ground almonds
- ♥ 1 tablespoon all purpose flour

Preheat oven to 400 degrees F

Cooking Steps:

1. In a medium pot, combine the pears and apples. Cook on medium low heat until tender about 20 minutes. Allow to cool in refrigerator for at least 1 hour.

2. On a lightly floured surface, roll out one pastry, cut it into four squares.

3. Spread a spoonful of almond paste in the center of each square and flat it. Place sliced pears or apples or mixed fruits on top to cover the almond mixture but leaving an half inch border; sprinkle raisins on top of the fruits. Brush the edges with egg wash, then fold pastry into a triangle; using a fork, crimp along the edges.

4. Make a slit in the top of turnovers, brush egg wash and sprinkle sliced almonds. Transfer them to the baking sheet, refrigerate for 15 minutes.

5. Bake for 15 to 18 minutes or until puffy and golden brown. Remove from the oven and allow to cool for 5 minutes.

6. Sprinkle with a little confectioners' sugar before serving. Serve turnovers with various berries.

7. Tip: to make a tart, leave pastry unfold in step 3, as an open phase pastry.

Almond Paste mixture:

1. In a bowl, with a wooden spoon, beat the butter and sugar together until light and fluffy.

2. Add the egg yolk and almond extract. Stir in the ground almonds and flour until evenly mixed. The mixture should be a thick paste.

Berry and Yogurt Parfait

Ingredients: *(makes 2 servings)*

- ♥ 1 cup homemade granola or store bought
- ♥ 1 cup fresh berries
- ♥ 1 cup fruit yogurt or vanilla yogurt

Homemade Granola: (*makes about 6 cups*)

- ♥ 2 cups old-fashion oats
- ♥ 2 cups unsweetened shredded coconut
- ♥ 3 tablespoons brown sugar
- ♥ 11/2 cups sliced almonds
- ♥ 1/4 cup of honey or maple syrup
- ♥ Pinch of salt.
- ♥ 1/2 cup cooking oil
- ♥ 1/2 cup dried fruits (optional)

Cooking Steps:

1. Pick your favor fresh berries, e.g. strawberry, blueberry, raspberry or blackberry.

2. In a serving glass, layer 1/2 cup of granola, a handful of fresh berries, and 1/2 cup of fruit yogurt, in order. Repeat layers and top with colorful berries.

3. Serve it with pancakes in breakfast or in desert.

Homemade Granola: (preheat oven to 300 degrees F)

1. In a large bowl, toss oats, coconut, brown sugar, and nuts with a pinch salt.

2. In a separate bowl, combine cooking oil and honey or maple syrup.

3. Pour the honey and oil mixture over the oats and nuts mixture, stir well until evenly mixed.

4. Pour onto a lined parchment paper baking sheet.

5. Bake for 30 to 35 minutes, stirring every 10 minutes to avoid burning, until golden brown.

6. Add dried fruits like raisins, cherries or cranberries, if you desire.

Chewy Walnut Squares

Ingredients: (makes 2 1/2 dozens)

- ♥ 2 eggs
- ♥ 1 cup brown sugar
- ♥ 2 teaspoons pure vanilla
- ♥ 1/2 teaspoon orange zest
- ♥ 1/2 teaspoon baking soda
- ♥ 1/2 teaspoon salt
- ♥ 1 cup all purpose flour, sifted
- ♥ 2 cups chopped walnuts

Preheat oven to 350 degrees F

Cooking Steps:

1. Greased a baking pan, preferably a square or rectangular size.

2. In a mixing bowl, use a wooden spoon, mix together eggs, brown sugar, orange zest and vanilla.

3. Quickly stir in flour, baking soda and salt.

4. Add walnuts; pour and spread into pan, evenly.

5. Bake for 22 minutes. Cookies should be soft in center when taken from oven.

6. Cool it, leave in pan.

7. Cut into squares; it makes 24 to 30 squares, approximately.

8. Refrigerate for weeks.

Cream Cheese Strudel
with Raspberry Sauce

Ingredients: *(makes 6 to 8 servings)*

- ♥ 8 ounces mascarpone or cream cheese
- ♥ 2 egg yolks
- ♥ 1 teaspoon vanilla
- ♥ 2 tablespoons flour
- ♥ 1 tablespoon lemon juice
- ♥ 1 teaspoon lemon zest
- ♥ 1/4 cup sugar
- ♥ 10 sheets Fillo dough
- ♥ 3/4 cup ground almond
- ♥ 3 tablespoons unsalted butter or vegetable oil
- ♥ 1 cup pecans or walnuts, toasted and chopped
- ♥ 1 cup fresh fruits for garnish
- ♥ Confectioner's sugar (optional)
- ♥ Raspberry sauce, recipe follows

Preheat oven to 400 degrees F

Cooking Steps:

1. Line a parchment paper on a baking sheet.

2. In a mixing bowl, beat egg yolks, flour and sugar, add mascarpone cheese, until smooth; drop lemon juice, zest and vanilla, mix it well.

3. In a small bowl, mix grounded almond with a table-spoon sugar.

4. Unfold the Fillo dough sheets and keep them covered with a damp towel. Brush first sheet with melted butter or spray vegetable oil and lightly sprinkle with ground almond mixture. Laying the second Fillo dough sheet over, brush with butter or oil and sprinkle with grounded almond mixture; continue the process until all 5 sheets are used.

5. Spoon cream cheese mixture along the center of pastry and spread the toasted nuts over; then fold either side of pastry over the filling. Roll and turn up side down, transfer to baking sheet. Continue to make the second strudel.

6. Brush strudels with butter and bake for 18 to 22 minutes or until golden brown and flaky.

7. To make the raspberry sauce: combine 2 cups fresh raspberries, 1 cup chopped strawberries, 1/3 cup sugar, 1/2 teaspoon vanilla, 1/2 lemon (juiced and zest), 1/4 cup water and 1 teaspoon brandy or rum (optional) in a saucepan and bring to boil then simmer until the sauce is getting thick. Press through a sieve and serve.

8. Using a serrated knife, cut strudel into 2-inch wide pieces; sprinkle with confectioner's sugar, if desired. Serve strudel warm. Garnish with fresh fruits and warm raspberry sauce.

Danish Pastry with Almond and Cream Cheese Filling

Ingredients: *(makes 8 to 10 servings)*

- ♥ 4 ounces cream cheese
- ♥ 4 ounces mascarpone cheese
- ♥ 1/3 cup sugar
- ♥ 1 egg yolk
- ♥ 2 tablespoons flour
- ♥ 1 teaspoon grated lemon zest
- ♥ 1 teaspoon pure vanilla extract
- ♥ 1 box frozen puff pastry, defrosted
- ♥ 1 cup almond paste (recipe Apple and Pear Turnovers)
- ♥ 1 egg, for egg wash
- ♥ 1 cup sliced almonds
- ♥ 2 tablespoons powder sugar
- ♥ Fresh fruits

Preheat oven to 400 degrees F

Cooking Steps:

1. Line a baking sheet with parchment paper.

2. For cheese filling, combine the cream cheese, mascarpone cheese, egg yolk, sugar, flour, lemon zest and vanilla in the bowl. Stir until smooth.

3. Take 1 sheet of puff pastry onto a lightly floured board; roll each side out slightly.

4. Spread 1/2 cup almond paste evenly to cover the middle third of pastry lengthwise into a wide strip; then, place the cheese filling over the top. Brush the border of each side pastry with egg wash.

5. Cut each side of pastry diagonally into about 1" wide and 3" long parallel strips from the edge of the filling. Fold one piece of strip over the filling, and then alternate with the opposite strip to the center; this cross overlapping stripes looks like a braid. Place the pastry on the prepared sheet pan.

6. Brush pastry with egg wash. Sprinkle sliced almonds over the top, evenly. Repeat with the second sheet of puff pastry and refrigerate for 10 to 15 minutes. Bake Danish pastries for about 22 minutes or until golden brown.

7. Let pastries cool before sprinkle powder sugar. Cut into strips to serve, garnish with fresh fruits.

Holiday Fruit Cake
With Pecan

Ingredients: (makes 1 big or 3 small loaves)

- ♥ 8 ounces candied cherry
- ♥ 8 ounces candied pineapple or colored fruits
- ♥ 1/2 cup brown sugar
- ♥ 3/4 cup flour
- ♥ 1 teaspoon grated orange zest
- ♥ 1 tablespoon pure vanilla extract
- ♥ 1 pound pecan nuts
- ♥ 1/3 teaspoon salt
- ♥ 1/2 teaspoon baking powder
- ♥ 3 large eggs
- ♥ 4 small baking loaf pans

Preheat oven to 300 degrees F

Cooking Steps:

1. Spray metal loaf pans with nonstick spray. Line each pan with parchment paper; cut the paper to fit, hang over the sides and ends, for easy removing. Spray oil again on parchment paper, set aside.

2. In a large mixing bowl, beat eggs and sugar, add flour, baking powder, salt, orange zest and vanilla and mix well.

3. Add colorful candied fruits and pecans into flour mixture and mix well.

4. Pour fruit cake mixture into loaf pans and press hard to the bottom and sides, no holes in between.

5. Bake for 30 minutes; turn the heat to 250°F, and bake for another hour or until golden brown .

6. Refrigerate for cooling, slice thinly and serve.

7. Fruit cakes can keep in refrigerator for weeks. They are best for hors d'oeuvres or snacks during Christmas or New Year holidays.

8. Tip: if you cut fruit cake thinly, it tastes very much like Chinese style pecan cake "核桃糕".

Mango Pudding

Ingredients: *(makes 4 to 6 servings)*

- ♥ 2 fresh mangos, peeled and diced
- ♥ 1 package unflavored Knox Gelatine
- ♥ 1/2 cup cold water
- ♥ 1/4 cup sugar
- ♥ 1/2 cup nonfat milk
- ♥ 3/4 cup Carnation evaporated low fat milk
- ♥ 1 teaspoon orange zest
- ♥ Colorful summer fruits, like blue berry or raspberry for garnish

Cooking Steps:

1. Prepare 6 (6-ounce) ramekins or one jelly mold.

2. Sprinkle gelatin over 1/2 cup cold water in a small sauté pan; let stand a few seconds and whisk to incorporate, about 30 seconds. Turn heat to medium high, add in 1/4 cup of the sugar and let it dissolved.

3. Pour 1/2 cup nonfat milk and 3/4 cup of the evaporated milk in the saucepan. Stir until well mixed. Add orange zest into gelatin mixture; bring to boiling, about 3 minutes. Then, turn the heat to low.

4. Reserve two tablespoons of mango for garnish, blend rest mangos on a medium-high speed until pureed, about 1 minute; the liquid is thick and smooth.

5. Pour the mango puree over the gelatin and milk mixture and whisk until well combined. Remove from the heat, let it cool.

6. Divide mango mixture evenly among the ramekins, or a large mold and refrigerate until set, at least 3 hours or overnight.

7. To serve, dip ramekin or jelly mold briefly in hot water then turn pudding out onto a plate. Garnish with mango bits or colorful fruits if desired.

8. Best serve within a day or two.

Orange Rolls

Ingredients: (makes 24 rolls)

- ♥ 4 cups flour
- ♥ 3/4 cup milk
- ♥ 3/4 cup warm water
- ♥ 1/4 cup sugar
- ♥ 1 package yeast
- ♥ 1 teaspoon salt
- ♥ 2 eggs
- ♥ 1/4 cup unsalted butter, melt

Filling:

- ♥ 1/3 cup sugar
- ♥ 1 teaspoon orange zest
- ♥ 2 tablespoons butter

Preheat oven at 375 degrees F

Cooking Steps:

1. Grease two 12-muffin pans, set aside.

2. For the filling, add sugar, butter and orange zest in a small bowl, mix well. Set aside.

3. For the dough, dissolve yeast in warm water; let sit until yeast starts to bubble. Beat 2 eggs, add sugar, salt and melted butter, stir in milk; combine them with yeast. Add 1 cup flour at a time, 4 cups total, mix them well. No need to knead, let rise to double the size, usually about two hours.

3. To make rolls, using a lot of flour on a working surface. Punch down and divide the dough in two. Roll out dough to the size of a rectangular,18"x 12". Spread 1/4 of filling down middle third of rectangular, the longer side; fold outer third over filling. Spread 1/4 filling over top of folded strip, then fold other side dough over filling. The strip should have the size of 6"x12", with three layers. Continue to finish second dough.

4. Cut each large strip into twelve 1"x 6" small strips and lay them on the floured board, gently stretch each strip out a bit then form into a spiral shape roll. Place them on greased muffin pans.

5. Let rise about 45 minutes. Bake until light brown, about 12 to 14 minutes.

6. To make orange glaze, combine 1/2 cup powder sugar and 2 tablespoons melted butter, add a little orange juice, just enough to drip from a spoon.

7. Ice each roll with orange glaze and serve warm.

Petite Blueberry Glaze

Ingredients: *(makes 9 to 12 servings)*

- ♥ 1 1/2 cups Graham Cracker Crumbs
- ♥ 1/2 stick unsalted butter, melted
- ♥ 1/2 cup sugar
- ♥ 1/2 teaspoon lemon zest
- ♥ 1/2 teaspoon vanilla extract
- ♥ 2 tablespoons sugar, divided
- ♥ 1 package (8-ounce) cream cheese
- ♥ 1 pint heavy cream
- ♥ 1 can (21-ounce) Comstock blueberry pie filling
- ♥ 1 cup walnuts, toasted and chopped
- ♥ Fresh blue berry or raspberry for garnish

Preheat oven at 350 degrees F

Cooking Steps:

1. Spray three mini 6-in by 3-in by 2-in (approximately) metal loaf pans with nonstick spray. Line each pan with parchment paper; cut the paper to fit, hang over the sides and ends for easy removing from the pan.

2. Mix graham cracker crumbs with melted butter and 1 tablespoon of sugar. Divide crumbs among three loaf pans; press each firmly, with a spoon, in bottom and 1/2 inch up sides of the pan. Place them on a baking sheet.

3. Bake 10 minutes or until golden brown. Let it cool completely.

4. Meanwhile, in a bowl, beat cream cheese, lemon zest, vanilla and half cup sugar until smooth (or mix with an electric mixer). Then divide and spread the cream cheese evenly over three baked crusts.

5. Chop walnuts, divide and sprinkle over cream cheese.

6. Beat half box of heavy cream with 1 tablespoon sugar until it forms soft peaks. Divide and spread whipping cream over walnuts.

7. To finish, spoon blueberry pie filling over the whipping cream. Shake it gently, refrigerate to chill for an hour.

8. To serve, lift the parchment paper from the sides of pan, carefully remove the paper and place onto a plate.

9. Cut into slices and garnish with fresh berries if desired.

Strawberry Banana Smoothie

Ingredients: *(makes 2 servings)*

- ♥ 1 banana
- ♥ 6 strawberries
- ♥ 1/3 cup fresh orange juice
- ♥ 1/2 cup crushed ice

Need a Magic Bullet or a regular blender

Cooking Steps:

1. Add all ingredients, strawberries, banana, orange juice, yogurt, and crushed ice into a blender.
2. Mix until smooth. Serve immediately.

Tasty Mixed Nuts Squares

Ingredients: (makes 2 dozens)

- ♥ 1 package Pillsbury sugar cookies dough
- ♥ 1/2 cup sweet orange marmalade
- ♥ 2 tablespoons honey
- ♥ 1 tablespoon lemon zest or orange zest
- ♥ 2 cups assorted toasted nuts, almonds, pecans, and walnuts
- ♥ 1/4 cup coconuts flakes
- ♥ 4 ounces semisweet white chocolate chips (optional)
- ♥ 2 tablespoons cream (optional)

Preheat oven to 350 degrees F

Cooking Steps:

1. Lay a parchment paper into 9-inch by 13-inch baking pan.

2. Place the cookie dough onto the baking sheet; slice the dough, lengthwise, into 6 pieces, spread them over the baking sheet. Lay another small piece of parchment paper or wax paper on top of the dough, then use the fingertips and palm to flat dough out evenly.

3. Sprinkle lemon zest all over, add handful almonds on top, and then press them down. Bake the cookie dough for about 22 to 25 minutes. Let it cool for 10 minutes.

4. Mix honey with orange marmalade, spread it over the cookie sheet.

5. Spread the mixed nuts evenly and press down the nuts to adhere to the orange marmalade mixture. At end, sprinkle the coconuts flakes over to cover the gaps.

6. Put back to oven and bake for another 10 to 15 minutes at 300°F.

7. Chocolate coating option: melt chocolate chips with cream in a glass bowl in the microwave with medium power for 1 minute, stirring until chocolate is melted and smooth. Drizzle melted chocolate on top of the nuts.

8. Let it cool in refrigerator for 45 minutes before cutting.

9. Cut the cookie into squares (a total of 24 squares); serve it with tea or coffee.

Vanilla Bavarois
with Strawberry Sauce

Ingredients: *(makes 4 servings)*

- ♥ 3 egg yolks
- ♥ 1/4 cup sugar
- ♥ 11/2 cups milk
- ♥ 2 teaspoons pure vanilla extract
- ♥ 1 package unflavored Knox Gelatine
- ♥ 2 tablespoons cold water
- ♥ 1 pint heavy cream
- ♥ 1/2 teaspoon cognac or other liqueur (optional)
- ♥ 1/2 cup fresh berries for garnish
- ♥ 1/2 cup strawberry sauce, recipe follows

Cooking Steps:

1. Lightly grease the bottom and sides of 4 (6-ounce) ramekin molds, chill in refrigerator. In a mixing bowl, beat heavy cream until it forms soft peaks, refrigerate before use.

2. Heat milk and vanilla in a saucepan over medium heat, remove immediately when it starts to boil. Let it cool.

3. Meanwhile, whisk the yolks and sugar until the mixture combines. Keep whisking and slowly pour in a bit of hot milk mixture to temper so the egg yolks won't curdle. Continue whisking and pour in the remaining milk mixture. Return to heat, stir until it thickens.

4. In a small pan, sprinkle the gelatin over the ice water and let stand a couple minutes. Turn the heat to low, stir gelatin until dissolved. Add the gelatin to milk mixture, stir well. Chill it in the ice bath, stir to make sure there are no lumps.

5. When the milk and gelatin mixture starts to set, add cognac and fold in prepared whipped cream. Spoon into prepared ramekins and chill in refrigerator for at least 3 hours or overnight.

6. To unmold, dip the mold in warm water for 10 seconds; then invert onto a serving plate. Serve Bavarois with strawberry sauce on the side and garnish with colorful berries, if desired.

7. For strawberry sauce, combine two cups sliced strawberries, 1/2 cup sugar, 2 tablespoons lemon juice, and 1/2 teaspoon lemon zest. Cook with low heat until smooth, about 15 minutes. Using a spoon, press through a sieve and serve.

A poem from the author's loving husband

精研中西烹飪術
融會貫通撰新書
傳統美食求改進
西洋名點加功夫
心靈手巧配佳肴
色香味全賽御廚
心得創意贈兒孫
慈暉留傳入食譜

美食是家庭聚心重要元素之一,烹飪技巧包括色香味的綜合及菜肴擺設的美觀,其境界昇華已進入藝術階段.培恩對烹飪及美食素有喜好,她集中西烹調技巧精研及健康易為的理念,改進及創新許多中式傳統食譜及西洋名點和菜肴.為了保留她的創見及心得,決定出書希望能留傳子孫,增進他們家庭和諧幸福及健康.這食譜是集合培恩精研健康美味而易為的中西菜肴並融進她對子女的母愛.同時希望給親朋好友分享她的心得與歷練.

The joy of sharing home cooked meals is one of the ingredients for a happy family. Skilled cooking requires a balance of tastes, colors, aromas and presentation.

Grace has always been fond of good food and the art of cooking. She has mastered Eastern and Western techniques and has merged traditional Chinese and popular American dishes into her own creations.

Her recipes are tasty, healthy, beautiful, and easy to prepare. She wants to pass on her recipes to her children, and hopes these healthy and delicious meals will enhance the health and happiness of their families.

This book has been a labor of love and she hopes it will be enjoyed by family and friends.

吾愛吾粹

雙雛嬉戲
丁巳年前日
吳門陸樹榮

Index

Index - 中國菜

Notes

Notes

Notes

More than ninety delicious recipes,
from traditional Chinese cuisine to
gourmet Western meals, that will bring
your family together any time of day.

$16.95 U.S

ISBN 978-1-4507-6395-

9 781450 763950